THE JOURNEY HOME

LUCINDA RACE

MC TWO PRESS

Manufactured in the United States of America Second Edition

Cover art by Meet Cute Creative
ISBN E-book 978-0-9862343-2-3
ISBN Paperback 978-0-9862343-1-6

Thank you for purchasing The Journey Home. I hope you enjoy reading Abby and Shane's story. I love writing characters who are a bit older and deserve a second chance at happiness. So, turn the page and fall in love in with the McKenna Family.

If you'd like to stay in touch, consider joining my Newsletter. I release it twice per month with tidbits, recipes and an occasional a special gift just for my readers.

https://lucindarace.com/newsletter/ and there is a free book when you join! Happy reading…

For my dear daughters, Megan and Emily, love will always bring us home.

For Rick, my sweet husband, you complete our family.

retrieve the cup on her way to the table. "I'd be happy to wash and refill it with apple juice. Maybe you'd like some tea?" She smiled at Abby who was patting the squirming, howling baby on her shoulder. "It's hard when they can't tell you what's wrong, isn't it?"

Abby, close to tears, looked up to see the woman give her an understanding smile. She was holding Devin's cup in one hand and a full coffee pot in the other. "Oh, thank you. I haven't gotten the hang of all of this baby stuff yet, and coffee would be wonderful." Abby was grateful she wasn't being asked to leave.

"Let me take care of the juice first, and I'll be right back." She retreated to the kitchen.

She returned in minutes with a plate of muffins, taking a moment to observe the girl and her baby. Abby was sure she could tell she was exhausted. The dark circles were a dead giveaway. She set the juice cup on the tray and the muffins on the table, then proceeded to pour steaming coffee into a mug.

Smiling, she asked, "I'm sorry, you look very familiar. Have you been in here before?"

"Mrs. McKenna, I'm Abigail Stevens. I went to school with Shane and Katelyn," Abby murmured.

"Abby, of course. I'm Cari Davis now; I remarried six months ago," she beamed. "Do you remember Jake Davis? He lived across our backyard?"

Abby nodded.

"I married his dad, Ray, on New Year's Day," she said with a twinkle in her eye. "Is this your baby?" Cari reached out to smooth the soft blond curls on his head.

"No, Devin is my sister Kelly and her husband Tim's son." Resting her cheek on Devin's head, her tears fell unchecked from her stormy gray eyes. "Well, he was," she added sadly. "They died in a car accident and appointed me his guardian."

Cari asked, "May I hold him?" She stretched out her arms. "Soon, I'm going to be a grandmother. Jake and his wife, Sara, are expecting twins."

Tear-free Devin leaped into Cari's waiting arms. To give Abby some privacy, Cari motioned for her to sit facing into the shop. She seemed to understand that sometimes a good cry helped more than anything else. She sat down in a chair, jostling Devin on her lap, and draped her arm around Abby. The soft sound of hiccups broke the silence.

Mortified, she croaked, "I'm so sorry. I can't believe I gave in to my pity party. Usually, I wait until the baby goes to bed. I'll take the baby monitor into the bathroom and cry in the shower until the hot water tank runs cold." Ashamed, Abby looked down at her clenched hands in her lap.

Gently placing her hand on Abby's arm, Cari attempted to reassure her. "It's okay. We all need to let go from time to time, and sometimes you can't help where or when it happens." She gave Abby's arm a pat. "Please, don't give it another thought. Besides, I got to hold this handsome young man." she grinned at the baby. "He is very sweet."

Abby lit up. "This is Devin Stevens Martin. Kelly didn't want her son growing up with a bunch of nicknames, so Tim said they'd better choose a name wisely. When Kelly found out she was having a boy, her in-laws insisted the baby have a proper family name. The Martin's weren't happy, but Kelly and Tim held their ground. Frankly, it was one of the only times Kelly didn't cave into their pressure tactics."

It was a relief to talk about her sister; since the funeral, Abby had felt lost and alone.

"I'm sorry. I hadn't heard about Kelly. Doesn't your family live outside of Boston? What brought you back to Loudon?"

Abby stared out the window. Her voice barely above a whisper, she said, "Loudon's always been my home. Growing up here was the best. I always thought, someday, when I had kids, I would raise them here. When everything changed for me, the only thought I had was getting away from the city and the sad memories. I wanted to open the back door and see green grass and breathe fresh air. I missed digging in the garden, and a little boy needs a sandbox and swings. I wanted Devin to grow up in the same house where his mother spent her childhood. So, I packed a few boxes, our suitcases, and here we are."

"When will your parents visit? I'm sure they miss you and Devin. Your parents were among the first to be regular customers when I opened the shop. "I'd love to see them."

Choking back fresh tears, she said, "It's just the two of us. My folks passed away before he was born. We're both orphans, facing the world together." Abby swallowed the lump in her throat. "Dad died suddenly; he had a massive heart attack. Before we had time to adjust, Mom was diagnosed with stage four cancer and, a few short months later, she was gone. And now our family has shrunk again." Abby toyed with a necklace that graced her neck.

"After the funeral for Tim and Kelly, I met with the lawyer and Tim's parents. I was shocked to learn Kelly and Tim had appointed me as Devin's guardian. Their will was very specific, right down to how their money was to be invested to ensure Devin's future. The Martin's were furious. They accused me of manipulating Tim. I tried to reassure them I had no idea about their will and that I would make sure Devin would spend a lot of time with them, but they stormed out of the meeting. I haven't seen them since. To be honest, with all that has happened over the last eighteen months, I didn't have the energy to deal with them. So, to make a sad story short, me and the little guy are starting over, in Loudon." Abby ran her hand over the baby's head and managed a smile for Cari.

Feeling drained, Abby took a sip of her coffee. It was cold by now, but she didn't notice. She desperately needed a jolt of caffeine to get through the rest of the day.

*C*ari's heart broke. Abby had suffered so much loss in a short time, and she deserved to cry for weeks. Sixteen years ago, Cari lost her husband Ben to a brain aneurysm, and she had cried for months. If it hadn't been for her friends and family, she didn't know how she would have made it through the darkest time of her life.

Cari's concern propelled her brain into overdrive. This young woman was alone, trying to deal with her grief and care for a baby without a support system. "Where are you living?" she asked.

"*L*ast week Devin and I moved into our old house on South Main. My parents never sold it as Mom always said this was where they planned to retire. We need to get a few things up-to-date before winter, but for now, we're comfortable, and it feels good to be home."

"Do you need any help getting things moved in or set up?"

"Thank you, Mrs. Davis; we're fine."

"As much as I love being called Mrs. Davis, Abby, my friends call me Cari." Her eyes twinkled.

"Right now, I could use a friend. Sadly, I've lost touch with everyone I grew up with." Abby wanted to kick herself. She couldn't believe she had said that out loud; it made her sound pathetic. She remembered that Mr. McKenna had passed away when she was a kid. If Cari could survive losing her husband and having to care for three children, she could certainly handle one little boy.

"For the next week or so, we're going to settle in. Then I need to find a job." Abby wouldn't admit she was overwhelmed by the work that had to be done on the house. For now, she had pushed the mental to-do list to the back of her brain.

The bell over the door jingled, causing Cari to glance up. Sighing, she held up a finger, indicating she'd be over shortly. "My husband."

"I guessed as much by the way he's looking at you." Abby looked at Cari, ready to cry again at the kindness, and then turned her attention to the baby. "Thank you for everything, Cari. Seeing you today confirmed I've made the right decision for both of us. Loudon is where we belong now." Impulsively, Abby threw her arms around Cari, squeezing Devin between them.

Caught off guard, Cari hugged her in return. "Why don't you and Devin come by tomorrow? Katelyn will be here and would love to see you, and we can have a late lunch together." I promise we won't throw temper tantrums or sippy cups across the room. I'm happy to hold this little munchkin so you can enjoy a peaceful cup of coffee."

Ray leaned on the counter and waited patiently. Cari

passed the baby to the petite brunette and laid a reassuring hand on the girl's shoulder.

"I'd like that. I'll see you tomorrow then." Abby secured a squirming Devin in his stroller and quickly gathered up the baby gear. She left the shop with a bounce in her step.

＊

Cari walked to her husband. Together they watched Abby through the front window as she headed to the south end of the street. "It's good to see you." She stretched up and planted a kiss on his lips. "What have you been up to today?"

Ray pulled her close. They had been married a mere six months, but it felt like they had always been together. Last year, Ray's ex-wife shot him. Luckily, she had been there, and with some quick-thinking Ray's injury hadn't been life threatening. She didn't want to think about how different the outcome might have been. However, it was also a blessing in disguise. During his recovery, they discovered they were in love with each other, much to their surprise. It had been a sharp reminder to both of them that life needed to be lived to the fullest.

"Who was the girl with the cute baby? She looks familiar, but I can't place her."

"Abigail Stevens. You remember the family that lived at the end of Main Street? They have that huge white house with the deep red shutters and black front door."

Ray said, "It's been closed up for quite a few years. I remember the family moved to Boston or someplace back east, but it seems they kept the house. It's been in their family for generations."

"Yes, she's the youngest girl. She and our three oldest kids went to school together. The baby is her nephew, Devin. She was appointed his guardian after her sister and her husband died in a car accident. Now, Abby has moved back to Loudon. She wants to raise Devin where his mother grew up."

Ray poured himself a mug and refilled Cari's coffee. "Is she married?"

She shook her head. "I don't think so; she said it was just the two of them."

"That's got to be hard, to change your life overnight and become a parent while dealing with the shock of losing your sister. How do you think she's doing?" Ray asked.

Cari frowned and drank some coffee. "Sadly, I think it's much harder than she expected. From what I can gather, her sister's in-laws have been giving her a rough time. On top of everything, Abby's parents passed away. Oh, Ray, it breaks my heart that she doesn't have anyone to lean on."

Ray tapped his finger on her forehead. "I see your wheels turning, and I get the feeling we're about to jump in before we're asked for help."

"Everybody needs friends. How many times over the years did you jump in and help me before I asked?" Cari cupped Ray's cheek in her hand. "I remember there were days I was so overwhelmed I didn't know what to do first, and then you would show up to lend a hand or just a little friendly adult conversation."

"Honey, of course we'll help Abby. That house has been closed up for quite a few years. I wonder if all the mechanical systems are working smoothly," Ray mused. He then pulled out a small notepad from his shirt pocket. Methodically, he started writing down items. Heating and hot water system were at the top of the list. "She doesn't need heat now, but it should be cleaned this summer."

Cari watched his list grow. She couldn't have married a nicer man, ready to lend a hand to anyone in need. She pulled him close to place a tender kiss on his mouth.

"What's that for?" Ray asked.

"You are the best man I know, and I love you," Cari spoke softly. "The smartest thing I've done in the last fifteen years was fall in love with you. If one of our girls was on her own, I hope someone like you would be there ready to help."

Ray kissed the top of her head. "Dear, I just follow your lead. You must have a plan."

"Kate will find out what Abby's plans are for the old house. Then the McKenna-Davis clan could pitch in to make sure she and Devin were comfortable and, most importantly, safe."

A customer walked in, interrupting Cari.

"Take care of business; I'm going to rally the clan and tell them we've got a new project." Ray moved from the counter and pulled out his cell phone.

She watched as he sent a text.

He gave her a thumbs-up.

Ray waited until Cari was free, then asked, "Ah, hon, the kids want to come for dinner tonight. Do we have anything we can throw together?"

She thrived on impromptu family gatherings.

"Sure, as long as you don't mind stopping at the store. Kate took the afternoon off, and I have to get a few things done before I close." Cari did the math in her head. "I think there'll be eight for dinner if Ellie doesn't bring a new guy with her."

She returned to what she was doing, thoughts drifting

to her youngest child, Ellie. She wondered how long it would take before Ellie was interested in a relationship. She had a lot of male friends and was always bringing someone home for dinner, but so far, that was all it was. Then her thoughts shifted to Shane, who would be flying solo, as usual. She worried about him the most. He dated lots of girls but kept everything casual. Shane reassured his mother that, when the time was right, he would find the right girl; he wasn't going to settle for second best.

Ray interrupted Cari's train of thought. "I just sent the kids a text saying dinner would be at seven. So, now I'm at your service. Just give me a list, and I'm off."

Cari jotted down a short note and handed it to Ray. Dinner would be a chicken and vegetable stir-fry with noodles and salad. He nodded with approval.

"Oh, and pick up some crusty bread too and maybe berries and heavy cream," Cari added.

"What, no biscuits?" Ray said in jest and put on a pouty face.

"I know, what are berries without biscuits?" Cari snapped her towel at him. "Off with you…"

*R*ay leaned on the counter, added bread to the list, and then tucked it into his pocket. He was anxious to drive by the old Stevens place and see how it was holding up. He could tell a lot from just looking at the outside of the structure. Tonight, he'd fill the kids in on what he thought would need to be done and, if he could see any structural damage, they could address that, too.

"I'll see you at home." Ray wanted to swing by Blake's Farmers Market to get the berries and vegetables and to buy some flowers to surprise his bride.

"You know, if you could hang around a little longer and watch the front, I could make biscuits."

Ray waved her to the back. "What I won't do for your biscuits, woman." He turned his attention to the pint-sized girl with a long brown ponytail who had entered the shop while holding tight to an older girl's hand.

Ray leaned over the counter. "Good afternoon, young lady. Do you see something you'd like?"

Ray pointed out various cookies in the case. He effortlessly handled other customers who came and went. He was comfortable swinging a hammer or selling coffee—completely at ease in their new blended lives.

It had been almost one year since a tree had fallen on Cari's house and demolished part of her home. Ray and their sons, Shane, Don, and Jake, worked to rebuild the sunroom, finishing right before Christmas. Cari and Ray had fallen in love and were married at the start of the new year. Now the newlyweds were redecorating her house to reflect their combined tastes. Ray's son Jake and Shane had been joined at the hip since childhood. Sara, Jake's wife, was a sweetheart. Cari didn't think of the kids as his and hers, but as theirs. Occasionally, it still surprised her that at this stage of her life she had been blessed with two more children and soon two grandchildren.

Cari's thoughts drifted back to Abby and the little boy who had been thrust together by fate. Someday, Abby would see this as a blessing. But for today and the foreseeable future, Cari and her family would do what they could to help her. Cari slid the biscuits into the oven and firmly closed the door. Tonight, would be a good start.

2

*T*he noise in the kitchen was deafening; six people were talking over each other, except for Sara, who was sitting quietly.

Ellie glanced at her sister-in-law and disengaged herself from the hubbub. She perched on the edge of the chaise lounge, where an uncomfortable-looking Sara was reclining.

"Here, Sara, let me tuck a pillow behind your back. It's going to be a few minutes before dinner is ready."

Sara leaned forward. "Thanks."

Ellie grabbed a couple of throw pillows and slid them behind Sara's lower back.

"Maybe this will make you more comfortable." Noticing her swollen ankles, Ellie added, "Do you want to slip off your clogs?"

Sara nodded. Ellie set them next to the chair.

"Thanks, Ellie. How do you always seem to know exactly what I need? You're going to be a terrific auntie to these two little ones."

Mom was telling everyone about Abby's sister, Kelly,

the car accident, and how she'd suffered the loss of her parents, too. Tears sprang to Sara's eyes as she listened. Ellie rubbed her hand as tears slid unnoticed down her cheeks.

In an attempt to distract Sara, she quizzed, "Are you getting nervous at all about the actual birth itself?"

Sara laughed nervously at the question. "I don't let myself think about it. The doctor says most twin births end up with a C-section. I'm hoping to deliver naturally, but as long as the end result is two healthy children, I don't care." Sara dropped her voice to barely a whisper. "Honestly, I can't wait till it's over. I've had enough of being pregnant, and I haven't seen my toes in forever."

Ellie suddenly had a brilliant idea. "Let's get pedicures next weekend? That way you can see your toes, and they'll be pretty for labor and delivery. *My* treat!"

Sara started to protest, "You don't need to spend your money on me."

Ellie held up her hand. "I bought the babies presents; this is *your* present."

Sara choked up. "I'm sorry for all the tears; everything makes me weep today, and that is the sweetest thing you've said to me, Ellie. And I'd love to get a pedicure. Let's make the appointment after I see the doctor tomorrow—just to make sure he's okay with it."

"Good, it's a date." Ellie was happy to see Sara perk up. "Afterward, if you feel up to getting a bite, I know a great place we can get a scone and tea."

Sara laughed. "That means we will be checking in with Cari and Kate. I can't wait." Sara leaned back and looked over at her husband. His attention was divided between his wife and the news that Abby Stevens had returned.

Sara gave him a thumbs-up and a big smile to reassure him she was fine.

"Cari?" Jake broke in. "Would it be okay if we didn't eat in the dining room tonight, but instead everyone can grab a plate and sit in here? I don't think we'll be getting Sara off the chaise right away—she's looking pretty comfy over there."

Mom glanced at Sara and at Ellie, who was keeping her company. "That's a great idea. We'll even deliver dinner to the two princesses over there." Mom gave Ellie a look that meant she should stay put so they could wait on Sara.

"Just like the old days. I was beginning to think you forgot that I'm the princess," Ellie piped up.

It was common knowledge that Sara didn't like to be fussed over.

"I know what you're thinking and you don't need to fuss over me. But how can I refuse Ellie when you're encouraging Cari? I guess I should enjoy it while I can. Before long, I'll be waiting on baby A and baby B."

Everyone chuckled.

Shane teased Jake, "Haven't you decided to tell us what they are yet, so we can start calling them by name instead of A and B?"

"My bride, who happens to be doing all the work, said this is the last great mystery of life, so we told the doctor that as long as they are both doing fine, we didn't want to know what their sex. Be patient; we'll find out soon enough." Jake draped his arm around Shane's neck and pulled him into an affectionate headlock.

"Here you go, Princess Sara and Princess Ellie," Mom teased as she delivered plates that were filled to the point of almost overflowing. Ray was right behind her with napkins and drinks, which he placed on a small side table he had slid next to the chaise.

"That's a lot of food." Sara moved slightly and placed a hand over her tummy. She grimaced. "They're pretty active tonight I guess they're ready for dinner," She shifted position again and balanced the dinner plate on her legs.

"It's mostly vegetables and they're good for all three of you," Mom stated. "So, eat up."

The family settled in various spots around the room, enjoying the meal and lighthearted conversation. Cari waited until there was a lull before speaking. "I'm glad everyone could come tonight. I'm sure you're wondering why we asked you to come over."

Shane gave his mother his full attention.

"As I have already told you, Abby Stevens was in the shop today with her nephew, Devin. Abby was awarded guardianship of and decided to move back to town to raise him here. Without a support system, I think she feels overwhelmed. So, basically, we need to see what we can do to help them."

Ray interjected, "I drove by her folks' house on my way home today, and the shrubs are severely overgrown and crowding the foundation. There are a couple of tree limbs hanging precariously close to the roof, and I saw at least one cracked window. That was all I could see from the street; I can't imagine what we'll find up close. So, who has a couple of hours on Saturday morning?" Ray glanced around the room. "I thought we could drop by, unannounced, and start working in the yard. Based on what your mom has said, Abby thinks she doesn't need help, but clearly, a few extra hands will make short work of the yard. While we're there, I'll poke around and see what else needs fixing."

"Dad," Jake spoke up. "I think this is a great idea, but I can't leave Sara, and she's in no condition to help."

"I've been thinking about that. Sara can keep Abby and the baby company and that way she isn't tempted to do anything. We're counting on her to find out what else Abby and Devin might need."

"Okay, that sounds better." Jake relaxed.

Everyone started off on side conversations while Cari noticed Shane was quietly contemplating the work.

"What time did you say Abby was coming into the shop tomorrow?"

"Around one, I think. She'll want to avoid the lunch rush in case Devin gets fussy," Cari replied.

"While she's with you, I'll swing by to scope out what needs to be done with the trees and shrubs to make sure we bring the right equipment. Don," he looked at his brother-in-law, "we'll be in and out before she gets back."

"Jason's crew is taking down those big pines at the Murray place in the morning," Don reminded Shane. "I don't want to leave the job site; the trees are really over-grown. It's going to be tricky bringing them down without damaging the house. Jason's a good supervisor, but he hasn't done a job like this before. One of us needs to be on site."

Shane ran his hands through his hair, thinking out loud he said, "Let's take both crews over there first thing in the morning. We'll get the trees on the ground and leave Jason in charge of the cleanup. He's good, and the worst of the job will be over before we take off for Abby's."

Don nodded his head in agreement.

Kate said, "The plans are coming together. We should

head over to Abby's around nine on Saturday and take a picnic lunch. When we're done, we'll have a 'welcome home' party for Abby and the baby."

"Great idea, Kate," Ellie chimed in. "I don't really remember her and it would be cool to get reacquainted."

"Then it's settled," Cari stated. "I'll see if Grace and Charlie can cover the store for the morning and they can join us for lunch. I hate to close before noon since there are quite a few people who like to pick up items for Sunday." Cari wasn't thinking about lost sales. For her, the issue was about being there for her loyal customers.

"Dessert anyone?" Cari asked as she moved toward the sink with a stack of dirty dishes in hand.

A chorus of "Yes" followed her as she crossed to the refrigerator. She opened the door and saw a small vase with a bouquet of wildflowers on the top shelf. Ray was watching her and she blew him a kiss from across the room as she placed the vase on the island.

3

*T*he level of noise rose in the great room as the family plowed through strawberry shortcake. Through the laughter and good-natured teasing, no one noticed that Sara was struggling to get up from the chaise until she doubled over and cried out in pain while clutching her midsection.

Jake rushed to her side. "Honey, what's wrong?" Slipping his arm around her he steadied her.

Shane quickly moved to her other side, supporting her.

A look of fear filled her face. "I don't know. I have a stabbing pain in my stomach that is moving around to my side. You don't think anything is wrong with the babies, do you?" Sara's voice was quivering near panic.

Cari had the phone in hand and was already dialing Sara's obstetrician as Ray rushed out of the house. He was getting the car. They weren't taking any chances. Sara was going directly to the emergency room to find out what was going on.

Shane and Jake were carefully guiding Sara to the door when she crumpled to the floor, crying out in pain. Don walked over and tapped Shane's shoulder, gesturing for him to step aside. "Hold the door," he said as he scooped Sara off the floor and rushed her to the waiting car. His long powerful strides eating up the ground.

"Jake, get in back. I'll slide her to you. Ray's driving you to the hospital. Cari called the doctor, and he'll meet you there."

Jake hesitated for a half-second, not wanting to let go of Sara's hand, but he ran around the car as Don said. Don gently bent down to the open door, treating Sara as if she would break, and passed her to Jake's waiting arms. The moment she was settled, Don slammed the door and rapped the window, signaling Ray.

Cari was in the driver's seat of her car, impatiently waiting for Ellie to get the seat belt buckled. Fear clutched her heart.

Shane leaned into the passenger door. "Mom, we'll lock up and meet you at the hospital."

*K*ate and Don were hastily wiping the counters when Shane called to them, "Ready?"

"Yes," Kate responded. "Shane, do you think Sara and the babies are going to be okay?"

"Kate, this is the first time any of us is having a baby, or in this case two. Maybe she's going into labor. If not, she's in the right place; her doctor will know what to do. They'll be fine." Shane held the door as Don and Kate went into the warm night air. He pulled the door firmly shut and turned the key. Despite his words of reassurance to Kate, he whispered a prayer for everyone to be fine.

It seemed like hours had passed since Ray had arrived

at the emergency room with Sara and Jake, but in reality, it had only been twenty minutes. A nurse met them with a wheelchair, and they eased Sara out of the car, being careful not to cause any additional pain. She was taken into an exam room where her doctor stood at the ready. Jake was escorted to the small waiting area. He was irritated about having to stand by and do nothing while his wife and children needed him. But the doctor was firm when he insisted. He needed to examine Sara without a nervous husband in the room.

Cari watched the exchange between her stepson and the nurse. Jake was too distracted to focus on the desk nurse. Cari walked up and gently guided him into the chair, and then rested her hand on his shoulder.

"Jake, you need to answer the nurse's questions. Something you tell her may help Sara and the babies."

She rubbed his shoulder as he turned his attention to the nurse while she moved through a series of questions about the last twenty-four hours.

"How was Sara moving around? Had she been eating? Did she fall? Had she been experiencing pain before tonight?" After each answer, she typed notes into the computer.

He shook his head. "Nothing has been out of the ordinary. She's been fine, resting and eating. I'm sure this is all necessary, but I need to be with my wife."

Cari didn't leave him, but she could see through the observation window into the waiting room that the family had arrived and settled in the hard, plastic chairs. They were ready to wait as long as it took to get answers.

. . .

*J*ust as the nurse wrapped up the questions and Jake signed for Sara to receive medical treatment, the doctor came to usher him into the exam room. He hesitated, looked at Cari, and then bolted through the door.

He was greeted by the sound of beeping monitors that were hooked to his lovely wife. He dragged his attention away from the monitors, anxious to hear the doctor's report.

"Dr. Thomas, what's going on? Is Sara going into labor?" He demanded.

"In layman's terms, after examining Sara, I believe she is suffering from severe gas pains. I'm not sure what she has had to eat today, but during the last few weeks of pregnancy, especially with twins, the uterus is going to grow quickly to make room for the babies. Pregnancy changes the hormone levels, and it slows down digestion. Sara needs to be careful about what she eats and to eat smaller and more frequently. This will help to alleviate heartburn and gas pressure." As Dr. Thomas explained, he started to breathe again for what seemed like the first time since Sara had doubled over.

"Are you sure she and the babies are going to be okay?" Jake desperately needed reassurance.

"We're going to keep her overnight, just as a precaution, but yes, the three of them are doing just fine. I promise you, if I had any reason for concern, I would tell you. Now, I'm going to arrange for a room upstairs. You're welcome to stay with her. I'll make sure they have a sleep chair by her bed.

"Thank you, Doctor." Jake moved to Sara's bedside.

"Would you find my family and give them an update? I don't want to leave her just yet."

Dr. Thomas smiled. "My pleasure, Jake."

Ellie and Kate were on their feet the moment they saw Dr. Thomas come toward them. Kate recognized him immediately because she and Sara shared the same doctor. The rest of the family gathered around him to get the update.

"Jake asked me to tell you the news. To put it simply, Sara is suffering from gas pains. I suspect that this might happen again as the babies take up more space. She is running out of room, and I don't think the babies are going to wait another four weeks before they make their appearance," he said. "I'm going to keep her overnight, as a precaution," he quickly added as he saw looks of relief replaced with concern. "Then tomorrow, I'm going to run a couple of tests to check on the babies and see how long we can wait before she can safely deliver. But I don't want you to worry. You did the right thing in getting Sara here quickly."

Ray put his hand out to shake the doctor's hand. "Thank you. I know I speak for all of us when I say Sara and the babies are in good hands."

"My pleasure. If you will excuse me, I need to make arrangements for Sara to be moved to a room. Currently, she's the only patient back there, so I don't have any objections if you all go in to see her before going home." Dr. Thomas moved to the nurses' station.

Without hesitation, the family filed through the swinging doors to see for themselves that Sara was feeling better.

Kate reached Sara first and kissed her cheek. "You

scared the daylights out of us tonight, chickee," she said, while also noticing how tired her sister-in-law looked.

Sara looked up, her cheeks flushed with embarrassment, and squeezed Kate's hand. "I'm sorry. It wasn't my plan. But I did find out that when I go into labor, I don't need to worry about getting to the hospital quickly. I think Ray set a new record."

Still blushing, she caught Don's gaze. "And, Don, I weigh a ton. You picked me up like I was a feather and then ran to the car."

"It was nothing, Sara. I've been practicing; I never know when I might have to rescue a damsel in distress," he teased.

The rest of the family crowded around the bed, talking all at once as they usually did.

After about ten minutes, Jake held up his hand to quiet everyone down. He stuttered, "Before they move Sara, we want to say you are the best family. What you did tonight means the world to us. Hopefully, the next time we do the mad dash, it will be to welcome the two newest members into the family." Overcome by emotion, he sank onto the chair next to Sara. She grasped his hand and gave it a reassuring tug.

On cue, the doctor pushed his way through the family to check on his patient.

"Sara, they're ready for you upstairs. Everyone can come back tomorrow. I would suggest that you all head home and let these two get some quiet time. Once babies A and B arrive, they won't have much time to sleep."

After exchanging hugs, the family filed out the door calling goodnight after them.

Cari took Ray's hand. "It's okay Grandpa. Everyone is fine."

He kissed her cheek. "Tonight, I was reminded how lucky we are to be a part of this family."

"We're all lucky." Cari slipped her arm around his waist as they walked to the car.

✻

*C*ari glanced up. To her surprise, Jake was ushering Sara through the door. Cari quickly slid around the counter to greet her daughter-in-law as she called out to Kate. "Sara and Jake are here!"

Cari smiled as she pulled Sara close. "This is a nice surprise. What are you two doing here?"

"I wanted to stop and pick up some lunch before I went home. The doctor ordered bed rest for the three of us. He is hoping to keep the babies percolating for a few more weeks. Every day gives their lungs a chance to get more developed."

Cari glanced at Jake, silently asking if there was anything to be concerned about. Jake gave her a slight shake of his head.

"So, are you feeling better?" Cari quizzed as she guided Sara to a chair.

"Yeah, I'm fine *and,* more importantly, the babies are fine. I have low-level toxemia. The doctor told me to drink plenty of water and avoid salty foods. And if I'm careful with what I eat, I should be able to avoid any nastier gas pains. Oh, and my blood pressure is a little high, so I have to take some pills for that. But otherwise, I'm good. Well, at least for a lady very pregnant with twins," she said with a laugh.

"I'll make you lunch and drop off a casserole for dinner

too, so you and Jake don't need to worry about fixing something later. I'm sure you're both tired after last night."

Kate had been standing by, listening to the exchange. "I can make some calls to our friends and arrange for people to look in on Sara while you're at work. This way you can get things wrapped up on the job you and Ray are working on before the little ones arrive.

Kate pulled out a chair and sat down. "You do look much better today than last night. You're actually glowing, Sara."

"Stop, I feel a little stupid, but physically I'm good. I hope the next time we check out of the hospital I can see my toes and have two new babies strapped into baby seats," Sara stated.

"For now, it sounds like you're going to be off your feet, and I know that you'll be going stir crazy, so we'll come visit and do our best to keep you from getting bored. I think that between Mom, Ellie, me, and, of course, the guys, we can keep you occupied for a couple of weeks."

"I don't want to be a bother to anyone." As tears threatened to spill down Sara's cheeks, she whispered, "It seems like over the last few months everything makes me cry."

Kate handed her a napkin and gently admonished, "Who said anything about being a bother?"

"Well, if everyone is rearranging their schedules to come over..."

Exasperated, Kate interrupted her before the thought was finished. "If the roles were reversed, and I was the one who was pregnant and needed rest, would you come over to keep me company?"

Dismayed, Sara answered, "You couldn't keep me away. We're family."

Kate let the statement hang in the air before responding. "Exactly, we're family."

The tears slid unchecked down Sara's cheeks.

"Okay, no more crying. It's settled. I'll grab a pad, we can make a list of things you need, and we'll take care of the rest."

After Kate found a pad and pen from behind the counter, the two girls put their heads together to make a checklist.

With Jake's help Cari packed a box with soup and fruit salad for lunch.

"Cari, thank you for all this," he said as he gestured to the overflowing box. "I can try and cook."

"Jake, you and Sara are a part of the McKenna clan, and this goes with the territory." Cari smiled at her stepson.

"Remember, there might come a day when you get tired of us hanging around, but that's part of the package, too," she said with a chuckle.

"I'll help you load this in the car, and you can get Sara home—she looks exhausted." Cari didn't want to come off as though she was being pushy.

"When you stop over later, would you mind staying for a while? I'd like to get the car and truck to the gas station, so they're both full. Just in case, well, you know. I might have to make a dash for the hospital and what if one vehicle doesn't start or something? I don't want to get caught off guard in case the babies decide to have their birthday early."

"I'm sure you'll be prepared when the time comes." Cari grinned at Jake. "I'm happy to stay for as long as you need me. It will give you a few minutes to clear your head, too." She tossed in a bag of cookies and said, "I'll carry this to the car. You can help your wife."

After depositing the box in the back and getting Sara situated, Kate and Cari stood on the sidewalk waving. "Call us if you need anything at all."

Cari slipped her arm around Kate's waist, pulling her close as they walked into the shop. "Are you okay, Katie?"

"Of course I am, why?"

Cari didn't want to bring up a painful subject. She took the hint, touched Kate's arm, and said, "All good things come in time, sweet pea."

Kate didn't reply to the unasked question as she made her way to the kitchen. "I need to take inventory and get the order placed before lunch," she said, closing the subject before it was opened.

Looking over her shoulder she said, "Let me know when Abby arrives. I'd love to see that adorable little boy."

$\mathcal{T}$he McKenna-Davis clan pulled up in front of the old Stevens place. Abby and Devin were likely inside because Abby's car was in the driveway and the baby's stroller was sitting outside the back door. Cari took the lead and knocked firmly. As the family waited in the yard, Shane, Jake, and Ray discussed what should be the first priority. Kate and Ellie stood guard over the coolers, and Sara sat in the car.

Abby swung the door open. "Hi, Cari. This is a nice surprise."

Kate and Ellie popped around the corner, carrying a couple of paper bags.

"Hey, Abs. We're your housewarming party on steroids." Kate laughed at the confused look on Abby's face.

"I'm afraid I don't understand. Please, come inside." She pushed the door open, leading the way into the sunny kitchen. Devin was strapped into his high chair, happily shoving pieces of squished banana across his tray and then into his mouth.

Cari took a couple of bags from Ellie after placing the potted plant on the back step. Kate dropped the last of the bags on the table. Ellie went to the car to help Sara as she waddled into the house. Curious, Abby trailed after Ellie to the front. She studied the four men discussing the branches that were touching her house.

Shane turned and his eyes came to rest on Abigail Stevens standing in front of him, hands on her hips.

"Um, guys, what are you doing?" Abby inquired.

This was not the scrawny girl who used to hang out with his sister. This girl was heart-stoppingly gorgeous. Her strawberry-blonde hair was cropped close to her neck, and fringe bangs graced her smoky gray-blue eyes. Abby had developed curves in all the places a man could use to hold her close. His eyes drifted to her deep red inviting lips. In his mind, he felt them yield under the crush of his mouth. His daydream was abruptly interrupted by a shove from Jake.

"Snap out of it, man, before she catches you staring," Jake whispered in his ear.

Shane brought himself back to the present and awkwardly stuck his hand out. "Hi, Abigail. I'm not sure if you remember me, Shane McKenna, Kate's brother."

"Of course, I do; you used to tease us every chance you got, and it's Abby." She reached out to shake his hand.

A shock ran through his body as their hands met. She withdrew it quickly and tucked it into the front pocket of her jean shorts.

"Hi, Abby. I'm Jake, and this is my dad, Ray Davis," Jake made the introductions since Shane was obviously tongue tied.

"It's nice to meet you, Jake. Your dad and I met the

29

other day at Cari's shop. So, what are you doing out here besides scoping out my trees?"

Cari and the girls came out to the porch just as Abby started asking questions. Sara settled comfortably onto the glider.

Cari walked down the steps and slipped her arm through the crook of Abby's. "The other day, you told me about moving back into your parents' place. After you left, Ray and I started talking about how long it's been closed up, and we thought you might be in need of a hand, or a bunch of hands, to get things settled. So here we are, just some old friends stopping by to help out."

Abby started to protest. "I appreciate you coming over, but the baby and I are fine. In a few weeks, I'll get everything organized, and we'll be in great shape. You're welcome to stay and have a picnic in the backyard, but please, I don't want anyone spending their Saturday working on my house." Abby looked around the group of familiar faces.

Ray stepped forward, "Abby, walk with me for a minute; I want to show you a few things."

Abby let herself be led away from the group. Cari was confident that Ray's quiet demeanor would work its magic and watched as Ray pointed from the trees to a couple of cracked windows, to the crumbling front walkway before disappearing around the back. After a short time, Ray and Abby were in the front yard again. Ray's arm was draped over her shoulders just as he did with Cari's girls.

She knew Ray had tactfully pointed out everything that needed to be done; it would take Abby forever.

But the turning point seemed to come when Ray had said, "A hand up isn't the same as a handout and remember to pay it forward when you can."

Close to tears, Abby accepted their kind offer. "It's the right thing for Devin, and now my life is all about that little boy."

Ray looked to his sons, "Boys, get the tools; there's work to be done and time's a-wasting."

Abby looked at Sara, noticing that she looked uncomfortable in the heat of the morning. "Let's get you into the house and in front of a fan. If you'll keep an eye on Devin, I'll put him in his playpen; then I can show you what I had planned to tackle first, that's if you want to help with the deep cleaning." Abby smiled at her oldest friend and her family. She could admit to herself it was good to be home and among friends.

Cari said, "I'm itching to work in the flower gardens. If Sara is content watching Devin while she obeys doctor's orders, Kate and Ellie can catch up with you while scrubbing windows and woodwork.

"A good plan." Abby smiled. "Ladies, shall we?"

$\mathcal{T}$he men got to work in the front, clearing away dead and hanging limbs and moved on to the stone walkway. Shane kept one eye open in hopes of catching a glimpse of Abby. He never thought the scrawny girl would have blossomed into one heck of a looker.

The sun hovered high in the sky. Abby had emerged from the house to check on the guys. A look of amazement was on her face as she watched as limbs were sent through the chipper, emerging as mulch. The pruning had opened up the front of the house, highlighting the shutters that were in dire need of a coat of paint.

Ray was on a ladder fixing a broken pane of glass. Jake and Shane had moved onto the front walk, laying displaced fieldstone into packed sand. Don had moved out to the side yard trimming overgrown hedges. Ray was right that this would have taken her months to get these things fixed if she could have done the work and that was if she had the extra money to hire someone. Shane heaved a large stone into place, his biceps straining against the weight. The sun was brutal and his light blue T-shirt soaked with sweat from exertion under the blazing sun.

*A*bby caught herself ogling him. Mentally admonishing herself to snap out of it, she took notice of the orange cooler under the tree. Despite the fact that she longed to watch him, pulling and pushing the stones into place, arranging the shapes and colors into a beautiful mosaic in the sand, she cleared her throat.

"Excuse me, guys? If anyone is hungry, we'll have lunch in about fifteen minutes. Come around to the back-yard where there is plenty of shade."

"Sounds great, Abby, I'm starving." Jake was anxious to check on Sara. "Yo, Dad," he yelled.

"Abby said lunch is ready. Finish up and come on."

Shane sat back on the heels of his work boots. He hadn't said much. He seemed to be half focusing his atten-tion on another piece of stone while his eyes followed her walking away.

"*H*ey, man, what is going on? You didn't say anything to her. She's so hot! You're the only single guy around here. At least you could be polite and say something. She's going to think you're a dumb jerk!" Jake shook his head.

"No, other than dinner at home and some time on the back deck, we're free. What's up?"

"Well...I was hoping you could babysit for Devin, Abby's nephew, just for a couple of hours. I'd like to take Abby to that new Italian place downtown." Shane paused, waiting for his mom to speak, but he didn't need to wait long.

"We'd love to take care of the baby. Does Abby mind if we take care of him at her place? That way she doesn't need to cart a lot of stuff around." He could hear that Mom was thrilled.

Shane pulled the receiver away from his mouth and whispered, "Here or at my mom's?"

"She will? Whatever is easier for them; they're doing me a favor." Abby grinned.

The pieces were falling into place for their date.

"Okay, thanks, Mom. I agree here is the easiest. Okay, talk to you tomorrow. Love you, too." Shane disconnected and slipped the phone back into his pocket, all smiles.

"All set. Mom and Ray will be over at about six. You can fill her in on the details about what time Devin eats dinner and any other baby-related stuff. At least that's what she said. And I'll pick you up at about six thirty? Mom thought maybe you would like to have some time to get ready without having to worry about Devin."

"That is so sweet of your parents. A few minutes to get ready would be a luxury I won't waste."

Devin started to fuss, and Abby glanced at her watch. "I didn't realize it was so late. It's time for Devin's nap. You're welcome to stay, but I'm sure you have other things to do."

Shane wondered why she kept saying he didn't have to hang around. Maybe she enjoyed her time when the baby was sleeping. "Sure, I need to get going. I have stuff to do at my place. I'll see you tomorrow."

"I'll be ready, and Shane, thanks, I'm really looking forward to our dinner." Abby walked into the house, cooing to the baby as she went.

Shane watched as the screen door closed behind her. He couldn't wait for tomorrow.

he morning flew by without a minute for Abby to check her closet for a suitable date outfit. She was starting to fret over what Shane would think when he arrived to pick her up and she was wearing shorts and a tee shirt. She wanted to knock his socks off, but the crazy day wasn't cooperating. Right after Devin went down for his afternoon nap, the doorbell rang.

Abby rushed to the front door only to discover the porch empty. Wanting to avoid waking Devin again, she raced to the back of the house, making a mental note to get the wiring fixed on the doorbells. She suppressed a giggle, remembering her dad had crossed the wires when he installed them. Hurrying through the kitchen, her bare foot stepped on something cold and squishy. She hobbled to the door, grabbed the knob, and flung it open with a thud. On the back step stood the McKenna sisters, wearing grins and holding garment bags.

"Is this a bad time?" Kate asked.

"No, of course not, come in." Abby wiped the sticky mess of old banana from her foot.

sandal that worked perfectly. The ensemble would be casual but elegant. Kate handed them to Abby.

Ellie draped the scarf around Abby's shoulders for the finishing touch. "This provides a hint of color and texture to the outfit and would serve to keep the chill away if the air-conditioning was too cold."

Abby turned to look in the full-length mirror. Once she fixed her hair and makeup, she knew this was the perfect outfit. She turned from her reflection, pirouetting in front of her friends.

"Well, what do you think?" It was the first time in weeks she felt almost normal.

With a nod of approval, Ellie laughed. "You'll definitely knock his socks off. I wish I could see his face when you answer the door."

Kate nodded. "He isn't going to have a single coherent thought in his brain when he sees you. Ellie, I think our work here is done. Let's have our tea before the little guy wakes up. Abs, Mom sent your favorite cookies, lemon drops."

"Are you sure you want me to fit into this dress tonight?" Abby joked. Her old friend knew anything lemon-flavored was a favorite indulgence.

The three girls laughed so loudly that Devin stirred. Abby pointed to the stairs and picked up the baby monitor as the girls tiptoed down the hallway. This was something she had sorely missed since giving up her apartment and life in the city—girlfriends, and girly stuff. Pleased she had rediscovered an old friend and made a new one, she felt her life was definitely on the upswing.

🍷

*a*t six on the dot, a knock came at the back door. Expecting Cari, Abby was surprised to see a large stuffed bear looking back at her. Cari and Ray peeked around the huge toy, grinning.

Abby reached to take the bags from Cari, while Ray wrestled the bear in through the doorway. "Cari, Ray, why did you bring that huge stuffed animal?"

"He's just a little something we picked up for Devin," he snorted. "I'm thinking maybe we, well, I got a little carried away. But isn't he soft? I bet Devin can sleep in his lap." Ray set the bear on a nearby chair.

She shook her head in disbelief. Devin was going to be spoiled rotten within a month. "That is very sweet of both of you but totally unnecessary. You've done enough for us already."

"That's the fun of it, Abby. Don't worry; we only do what we want to do. Isn't that right, sweetheart?" Cari flashed her husband a sweet smile.

Ray laughed. "To be honest, you lead, and I follow. It's more fun that way."

Cari bussed her husband's cheek. "Now, go get all dolled up. Ray and I have everything under control. Shoo." Cari waved her hand toward the stairwell, dismissing Abby.

"Devin's in the playpen which I have set up in the living room," she called after them. "Make yourself at home." Talking to an empty hall, she glanced at the clock. "Gosh, Shane will be here in twenty minutes." She flew up the stairs.

Cari leaned over the play area and scooped Devin up, talking to him in hushed whispers. Ray waited while Cari drank in her fill of this sweet baby smell before nudging her. "It's my turn now." He stretched out his arms to take Devin, who all but leaped into his arms.

She glanced out the front window when she heard Shane pull up, relieved to see his convertible instead of his truck. She heard footsteps on the stairs and turned in time to see Abby reach the bottom step.

Ray smiled warmly. "Abby, let me be the first to say how beautiful you look tonight, and if Shane doesn't say anything for a few seconds, it's because he forgot how to speak."

She blushed, and her eyes sparkled. Cari crossed the foyer and whispered in her ear, "My son is a very lucky man to have you on his arm tonight. I hope it is the first of many evenings together." Cari gave her a peck on the cheek just as the knock came at the door.

Ray and Cari retreated into the background; they wanted to see Shane's reaction but not intrude on their moment.

Shane was inspecting his shoes as Abby swung the door open. Slowly his gaze slid up from her pink toenails, taking in her lightly tanned legs, to the hem of the lavender dress, to the hint of creamy skin gracing the neckline, following the waves of strawberry blond hair that framed her chin. A smile played across her pink gloss-coated lips until finally, his eyes found the smile in her deep velvet gray eyes. "Abby, you are so beautiful," Shane said huskily.

He watched as Abby's cheeks went bright pink. She blushed under the intensity of his gaze. If she had wanted a reaction she certainly got one. He continued to watch as it was her turn to take a good look at him. He stood before her in dark navy-blue dress pants, an ivory button-down shirt, open at the throat with the cuffs turned back, exposing his deeply tanned forearms.

"Thank you; you're looking pretty good yourself," she answered back. The baby giggling in the background reminded Abby and Shane that they weren't alone. "I'm ready to go if you are?"

"Lead the way." Shane wanted to follow her anywhere, but dinner was a good place to start.

Abby turned to Cari holding Devin. "You be a good boy." She leaned over and kissed the top of his head. "If you need me, my cell number is on the table, and of course you have Shane's."

"Go and enjoy your evening. Everything is under control." Cari gave Abby a gentle prod toward the door. "Take as long as you like."

"I guess I'm a little nervous. This is the first time I've left him with anyone." With one final look over her shoulder, Abby glided down the walkway to the car. Shane pulled open her door before going around to the driver's seat.

The engine rumbled to life, and Shane dropped the car into drive. "I hope you're hungry. I've heard the food is great and there'll be plenty of it. Don and Kate went there right after it opened." Shane grew quiet on the short drive. Now that he was alone with Abby, he wasn't sure what to talk about. He slid the car into a parking space a couple of blocks from the restaurant. "Are you up for a short walk?"

"Sure, it's a lovely night."

She waited for him to come around and open her door. He offered her his hand as she slid out of the low-slung seat. Abby decided a Porsche was a great idea if you weren't wearing heels and a dress.

As they strolled down the sidewalk, wonderful aromas mingled in the flower-scented evening air. They walked into the courtyard. Shane nodded to a few people he knew and approached the host's station. Finding their reservation, the host gave them a choice of the courtyard or the dining room. Hesitating, Shane looked at Abby. "Lady's choice."

"The courtyard would be lovely, but you work outside in the heat, so maybe you'd prefer the cool comfort of the dining room?" Abby's nerves were in overdrive. Before her knees gave out, she wanted to sit down.

Shane told the host, "Courtyard, please. Do you have a quiet corner table?"

"Certainly, sir. Right this way." The host moved ahead of them, holding the door for Shane and Abby and ushering them to a table for two. "Will this be okay?"

Shane nodded as the host held out a chair for her. "Your waiter will be right with you," he said before making a discreet exit.

"We should have sat inside. It's very warm tonight, and I'm sure you'd be more comfortable."

"Honestly, I prefer to eat outside. The summer goes by quickly, and as you know, the winters are long and cold around here."

The couple was at a loss for words and silence crept over the table. Thankfully, the waiter came to take their drink order. After a short debate on the merits of white versus red wine, they decided to share a bottle of Merlot. Abby thought the fact that she was experiencing butterflies was crazy, considering she had known Shane for most of her life.

· · ·

*D*etermined to break through the uncomfortable silence, she said, "I was surprised to see you still have the Porsche. I remember when you brought that junk heap home. I thought Cari was going to kill you."

Grinning with pride, he said, "Yeah, Mom wasn't happy, but I've tinkered with it ever since, restoring it little by little. It sure wasn't pretty when I brought it home, but now it runs like a top and looks sharp, too."

"What made you decide to get into the landscaping business? In school, you mowed lawns and did odd jobs, but I thought you would go to college and be a doctor or something. As I recall, you were a science nerd in school."

Shane visibly relaxed. "I *do* love science. In our senior year, I got accepted to Boston University. I couldn't stand the thought of eight-plus years of more school or living in the city. I didn't want to be cooped up in a classroom. I liked being outside and had been mowing lawns since I was about thirteen. When I started driving, I got a few more lawns, and the money was really good. So, I made a deal with my mom. I decided to take a year off from college and see what type of business I could develop. Obviously, summer is the easiest because grass grows constantly."

Shane laughed. "That was a stupid comment. So, anyway the deal was, if I had a good customer base and was turning a decent profit, I could take my college fund, invest in more equipment, and hire people. Of course, my mom made me write a business plan first. That first year, I worked my butt off, and to everyone's surprise, I turned a nice profit. I appreciated that people put their trust in me. The next winter, my mom and I evaluated the numbers, and she agreed that I could use a small portion of my college fund. To be honest, I think she was worried the first year was a fluke, or that I'd get tired of the physical work. By the end of the second year, I discovered I had a good head for business. A couple of years ago, I hired Kate's husband, Don, and the business has continued to expand. Now, I think it's time I hire an office manager. We have so much work that I need to be in the field—to keep the crews going, and besides, I like working outside much better. I don't have time to keep up with office work and return calls at night. Suffice it to say, I have no regrets with my choice."

In the middle of his story, the waiter had interrupted long enough to get their dinner orders. By the time Shane had finished, the waiter was delivering their main course.

"Your mom is a smart lady. You got to test the business waters and still give yourself a fallback position if you ended up wanting to go to college. Physical work isn't right for everyone, and on top of that, you now run a very successful business. I have to admit, I'm impressed. Your business has grown quite a bit relatively quickly. Do you think you'll continue to expand or are you satisfied with the business for now?"

"I don't have any active expansion plans, but the most important lesson I've learned is to expect the unexpected opportunity. So, who knows what will come up next?" Shane sat back and watched Abby dig into her pasta. It was a refreshing change to see a girl eat instead of pretending to and push food around her plate.

"So, what about you, what happened after your family moved to Boston?" He hadn't given much thought to his sister's childhood friend until a few days ago. Suddenly, he wanted to know everything. That was an understatement, for some reason he needed to know everything.

"It's quite simple actually. My dad had a great opportunity with his company—huge salary increase and benefits. Kelly was in school out there but was having a hard time with apartment living, roommates, and all, so our dad decided to take the job, and we moved. But Mom missed her friends from here. To meet people, my mom did substitute teaching. More than anything else, working was a social outlet for her. I finished high school and, during my senior year, I took a few college-level courses to get a jump start in college. I had a full course load, did summer semesters, and was able to finish up in just about three years. I guess I did the ultimate fast track of college. Most people seem to do the five-year plan, I did it in three." She took a sip of her wine. "Anyway, I graduated with a teaching degree in fine arts. I was working with a youth program, teaching art part-time, and I also worked in an art supply store. I didn't know what I wanted to do when I grew up." Abby laughed at herself.

"In the meantime, Kelly met and married Tim. They had just announced the news about being pregnant, and everything started to crumble. My dad had a massive heart attack and died. Before we had time to finish grieving, my mom was diagnosed with stage four ovarian cancer. She didn't show any symptoms until it was too late. One night, I was sitting with her, and she told me, Kelly and I would have to take care of each other. She died about a month before Devin was born. She fought so hard, but I think losing Dad sapped her will to fight. In the span of six months or so, we went from a family of four to two. Tim was wonderful to both of us. When Kelly had the baby, it was a blessing, but a bittersweet reminder of how precious life is." She paused, feeling the pain of loss again. She felt compelled to tell Shane everything, to share with him why having Devin was the only choice for the both of them.

Abby spoke softly when she continued. "I encouraged Kelly and Tim to have a date night. Tim had arranged to take her to this little B&B that she had fallen in love with when they were dating. I was happy to step in and babysit for the weekend; Devin was such a good baby. When Sunday night came, and they hadn't called, I wasn't worried. I figured they wanted to squeeze out every moment they could before coming back to the city. I'll never forget the split second our lives changed; I was in the family room watching TV, and the baby was sleeping. I heard a car pull up and the doorbell ring." She wiped a lone tear from her cheek. And then she swallowed the lump in her throat. "I remember thinking it was odd that I hadn't heard the garage door open. I opened the door and saw two policemen on the front porch. Without missing a beat, they asked me my name and my relationship to Kelly and Tim. As soon as the words left my mouth, they asked if they could come inside. I held the door open, cold air rushing in behind them. I knew whatever they were going to say was going to be bad, really bad. When they informed me about the car accident, I don't think I cried; I was numb. I remember asking if Tim's parents had been notified. They said no and asked if I would like them to handle it. I didn't want them to get the news the same way I had, and so I said I would call them. The week that followed was a blur. I have never felt so isolated and alone. When our parents died, Kelly and I had each other for support. The only person I had left in the world was Devin."

. . .

"*B*ut you had Tim's parents, and what about his brothers and sisters? Weren't they there for you?" Shane wanted to wrap his arms around this incredibly resilient woman and take away every moment of pain she had felt.

"Tim was an only child, and his parents are cold as ice. They're concerned with appearances. I let them take care of the funeral arrangements. I didn't care what they planned. Then, at the reading of their wills, things went from bad to worse. Kelly and Tim left very specific instructions. I was appointed full custody of any and all children, and I was to oversee the finances. Tim was a trust fund baby and had a good job, so there were investments. His parents were furious. They demanded their lawyer contest the will. Tim's best friend, Kyle drew up Tim and Kelly's will, and I think that ticked them off too since Tim didn't use the Martin's' family lawyer. It was a nasty mess, but thankfully it's behind us. In a few weeks, I'm taking Devin to Boston for a weekend visit with his grandparents. It's good for them to see their grandson and vice versa." She released a deep sigh. Her soft gray eyes met his. "I sound like I'm whining."

Abby didn't realize her face was wet. Shane reached across the table and gently wiped away her tears with his handkerchief.

"Not at all. I am sorry you had to go through so much by yourself. But you're among people who care about you and will help in any way we can. You and Devin aren't alone anymore," he reassured her.

She gave a gentle smile. "It seems your family has adopted us and I'm feeling better about our future every day."

dips with each contraction. So rather than wait and see what happens, our doctor feels the best thing to do is take Sara in for surgery now." Jake paused, his brow furrowed with worry.

Cari crossed the room. "It's hard to be the observer but try not to worry; it's the best option for all of them." Cari hugged Jake. "Are you going in with her?"

Ray rested his hand on his son's shoulder. "Everything will be fine, and before you know it, you'll be a dad."

"Yeah, I know. I need to get dressed in scrubs, so I can be with her. They didn't say how long it would take to deliver the babies, but I'll be back as soon as I can." He hurried off and turned on his heel. "I'm glad you are here. I feel better knowing our family is close by."

*D*ressed in pale green scrubs and a matching hair cap, he was escorted to the operating room. Sara lay on the table, the large mound that was her stomach draped in a huge sheet. Dr. Thomas and an assisting surgeon entered. He watched the nurses arrange bassinets and various instruments that might be needed. Jake decided the less he knew, the better.

Sara stretched her hand toward him. A solitary tear slid from the corner of her eye sliding downward. Jake grasped her cool hand, rubbing warmth into it. He leaned over and spoke in a reassuring voice. "The family is here, and I've called your parents. They can't wait to meet the babies." Jake wished he could trade places with her, but the most he could do was stay by her side. "Are you in any pain, honey?"

With a trembling voice, she answered, "No pain. You called my mom and dad?"

"Of course, I did. I'm sure by the time we're parents, their suitcases will be packed, and they'll have plans to head our way."

Sara couldn't tell but he was grinning behind his mask. She focused on his hazel eyes. She gave his hand a tug. "Thank you for being the best husband. You know our life is about to change drastically..."

Jake and Sara's conversation was interrupted. "Well, Sara," Dr. Thomas said. "Are you ready to meet your children?"

"I'm ready," Sara piped up.

"Okay, let's get the show on the road." Dr. Thomas's tone was light. He turned to his team, accepting instruments and working behind the draped fabric. Everyone worked in perfect synchronization. The doctor nodded in the nurse's direction, and she confirmed she had a blanket ready.

"Note time, eleven-thirteen baby A." He looked up briefly. "Sara, Jake, you have a handsome little boy." The doctor stopped talking then, concentrating on his patient instead.

Jake and Sara grinned at each other as the first cries from their little boy pierced the room. Another nurse stood ready. Eleven-sixteen, baby B, a beautiful girl. Time to finish up." The doctor paused. "Ah, what is this?"

Sara raised her head, straining to see what was going on. "What's wrong?" she demanded, panic creeping into her voice.

"Well, it seems we have a bit of a surprise; there's another baby. Another boy. He's small but looks perfect in every way. Congratulations, you two, I can safely say you're going to be pretty busy."

The delivery room was filled with people murmuring

stats and babies crying, irritated to have been thrust into the world.

Jake was stunned. Sara grinned at him. "Well, you said you wanted lots of children. Looks like you got your wish."

His knees were knocking. If he hadn't been sitting on a stool, he would have fallen over. "Can we see them?"

"As soon as they are checked over and cleaned up." Dr. Thomas whistled a little tune as he finished whatever it was he was doing.

"Sara, we don't have enough room." His voice sounded strained. "We're going to have to add on to the house. They're going to need their own bedrooms, and we're going to need another bathroom." Jake's brain was whirling faster than he could speak.

"Jake, honey, we have plenty of time. Right now, they're little tiny babies. Breathe. We'll cross that bridge when we need to. At the moment, all I really want is to see our children before I go to my room."

Sara struggled to see what was going on with her babies but lying on an operating table, hooked up to IVs and monitors, wasn't conducive to a clear view. A nurse appeared on her left.

"Sara, are you ready to hold a baby?"

Sara nodded. "Absolutely." Her eyes wide with wonder.

"Here's your little boy, Baby A." The nurse tucked the tiny red-faced baby in the crook of his mother's arms. She gazed at the baby, love struck. She looked at Jake with tears filling her eyes.

"Jake, would you like to hold your little girl?" The nurse repositioned his arms to cradle his daughter. He was speechless, staring at the sweet face looking up at him.

"Sara, here is Baby C; he's tiny but strong. He did well on the Apgar, like his brother and sister." She stood where Sara could take a good look at him.

"Can I hold him, too? He's so small, but I need to hold him, he's our bonus baby."

"Of course, you can hold him." The nurse placed him on Sara's other side. "I need to get them upstairs to the nursery, but you can definitely have a few minutes."

Jake and Sara kissed and snuggled each bundle of love and then reluctantly passed the babies to the nurse. After tucking them into the waiting bassinets, the nurses whisked them from the room.

"Jake," Sara urged, "go tell the family our news, and I'll see you upstairs."

Reluctantly, he started to leave, and he was partway out the door when he turned back, slid his mask down, and placed a loving kiss on his wife's lips. "You are an amazing woman, and I love you. Thank you for giving me three beautiful children," he said and then he felt like he floated on air to the waiting room.

Ray took a good look at his son. "You look very happy." He enveloped Jake in a bear hug. Cari waited by his side. Overcome with emotion, Jake broke down and wept in his father's arms.

"We got a little surprise in the delivery room." Jake waited for half a beat before continuing. "Baby A is a boy; Baby B is a little girl, and…" He paused, taking a deep ragged breath, and then said, "Baby C is a little boy."

"Oh, my stars, three babies?" Cari exclaimed, clapping her hands with delight.

Everyone started talking at the same time, bombarding Jake with questions.

He held up his hands. "Before I answer, here's what I

can tell you. Everyone is fine. Sara did great and can't wait to see you all. Baby C is small, and for a while, he'll need special attention. If you're ready, let's go meet my children." Jake turned. "I hope you don't take this the wrong way, but can you poke your head in to see Sara and then head home? She's had a pretty eventful day, and I'd like for her to get some rest." Jake didn't wait for an answer as he walked into the elevator.

"When do you think I'll be able to hold my grandbabies?" Ray asked, knowing the question was on everyone's mind.

"I'm sure you can see them, but I don't know when you can hold them, maybe tomorrow." Jake thumped his father on the back, hooked arms with Cari, and stepped out of the elevator. "Come on, Grandpa and Grandma."

The proud father led the way. Seven people lined the large glass-covered wall of the brightly lit nursery. Three isolates with precious miracles stood in the middle of the room. A pediatric nurse came to the door. "Mr. Davis?"

Jake showed his wrist bracelet and was escorted into the room. He grinned to his family. He didn't want to waste a single minute. The nurse had him scrub his hands and put on a fresh gown. She picked up Baby A and placed him in Jake's arms. She repositioned his arm to support the baby's head. He walked to the glass, proudly showing off his son. He stood in front of each family member, looking like he had been holding babies all his life.

"Jake's a natural, but to witness this transformation is a gift." Cari slipped her arm through Ray's. "I'm so grateful we're all together to share this very special night."

Jake reluctantly put each baby down, placing a tender kiss on the tops of their heads. Before leaving the nursery, he took one last look and said a silent prayer to protect his children while they were away from him. He wanted to check in with Sara and then get some rest. Exhaustion was setting in.

He came out of the nursery. "What do you think? We did good, right?" He glanced at everyone. "Let's stop in and check on Sara, and then I'm going to head home." He looked at his family. "Shane, would you mind driving me? I don't think my eyes will stay open."

"Consider it done. Take Mom and Ray down to see Sara. Give her our love, and we'll wait here." Shane pushed his brother down the hall towards his wife's room.

"Sara?" Jake whispered while tiptoeing to her bedside and then taking her hand in his. He dropped a gentle kiss on her lips. Sara's eyes fluttered open, and she smiled at her husband.

"Hi, Daddy. Have you seen them?"

"Yeah, I showed them off to the family. They're all tucked in for a while. Dad and Cari are here."

She looked around the semidarkness. "Hi, Dad, Cari."

"Hi, kiddo. You did good today." Ray gently rested his hand on her arm. "We wanted to see you before we go home and to let you know we'll be back tomorrow."

"Sara, the babies are beautiful, and they look just like their mom." Cari brushed Sara's hair off her face. "Get some rest."

She was fighting to stay awake. "Take Jake with you? He's exhausted." Drifting off, she said, "Go home, honey, and sleep. It will be one of the last quiet nights for a few years." A smile played across her lips as she zonked out.

Jake obliged and leaned over to kiss her again. "I love you, Sara. Sleep well."

LUCINDA RACE

Her rhythmic breathing reached his ears before he reached the door.

"Thanks for the offer, Cari, but you have done enough. We'll be fine tonight. My mom is due in tomorrow, and we have a baby monitor in our room. The kids will sleep in their cribs. Between the two of us, we've got it covered." Sara did her best to sound confident.

"Well, if you change your mind and need reinforcements, Dad and I are ten minutes away, and we're happy to come help. I remember what it was like the first night we brought the twins home. Ben and I wanted to be alone with them, too. It was rough the first night, but I wouldn't have changed a thing. It was the start of our family." Cari reached over and pushed a lock of hair out of Sara's eyes. "So, when I say I understand, I do."

Sara hesitated. "I do have one favor to ask. Would you mind watching them while I take a shower? I'm not sure Jake's ready to be alone with them yet."

"Of course, take your time." Cari patted her hand. "I'm happy to be a doting grandma for a little while longer."

"I won't be long," she called as the bathroom door closed behind her.

Kaylee started to fuss. Cari scooped her up and went into the kitchen to warm three bottles. It wouldn't be long before the boys would be awake and hungry, too. She prayed their family continued to grow, but hopefully the next pregnancy would produce one child, not three. As she looked from one bassinet to another, the two little boys began to stir. In the coming months, the entire family was going to have their hands full. Before she could call out, Kate and Ellie appeared, wiping their hands on a towel.

"Sounds like you need some help in here. We left Don to finish up." Ellie bent to scoop up Zach, and Kate did the same with Brad. "Mom, you're going to need to teach diaper changing; someone has a stinky one." Ellie wrinkled her nose up as Cari broke out in a belly laugh.

"Aunties, since babysitting was never part of your teenage years, here's diaper lesson one-oh-one: first, find a good place to lay the baby down and make sure it's on something that is washable..." This was a first for both of them.

9

*S*hane was planning on taking a few days off to go to Boston with Abby. While he was gone Jake was going to step in and help out with a work crew. Although life quickly developed into a rhythm for the new parents the babies were settling into a routine and Sara's folks were in town indefinitely. With space at a premium at Jake's, Sara's parents were staying at Ray's old house. Working for his dad made Jake's schedule flexible, so pitching in on any of the family businesses just happened. It helped Shane feel like he hadn't dumped a lot of extra work on Don.

Abby was watering the flower garden when Shane snuck up behind her. "Hey, the flowers are looking good."

Startled, Abby looked out from under the large brim of her sun hat and flashed him a welcoming smile. "Hi there. How is everything with the new parents?"

"Everyone is doing great. Sara's parents are here, so everyone seems to be getting some sleep." Shane dropped a chaste kiss onto Abby's cheek. "Where is the little guy, swinging in the trees?"

"Still sleeping, we had a busy morning. We took a walk to the park and then played in the backyard, so he got tuckered out."

"You do a great job with Devin. After seeing Sara handling the little ones, I'm impressed by all mothers." Shane reached out to tuck a stray lock of hair behind her ear. "Did I tell you Sara named the little girl Kaylee? She combined Kate and Ellie's names. My sisters were touched."

"That is so sweet. Sara seems like a nice girl and a good match for Jake."

"He got lucky when he met Sara. Have I ever told you how they met?"

Abby shook her head.

"We went to Maine for the weekend. Thought we'd hang out at the beach, catch some rays. We were playing volleyball, and he literally tripped over her. He dove for the ball and fell over her, spraying sand everywhere. When he saw how beautiful she was, he begged her to have an apology drink. After she got done being mad, she agreed, and that was all she wrote. They've been inseparable ever since." Shane grinned.

Abby was laughing hard. "I don't know if some guy tripped over me if I'd agree to have a drink with him. He did get lucky."

"Well, I didn't stop to bore you with old family stories. I was wondering if you've figured out what time you're taking Devin to his grandparents."

"Friday, midday. It will take about three hours door to door depending on traffic. I'll get him settled and come home later that same day. Then Monday I will go pick him up. I had hoped that Tim's parents would meet me halfway, but they don't want to make it easy for me. Even though it's a lot of driving, he needs to see his grandparents." Abby gave an off handed shrug. "So, I'll do what I have to do."

"Since you're going to be free for the weekend, how about you come out to my place on Saturday? I bought the old McIntyre house on Green Lake. We can take the boat out, swim, and grill up some burgers and just chill. Or we can do something else if you prefer. Your choice." Shane didn't want her to get the wrong idea. "Strictly platonic, we can pick up our conversation from the other night." Although seducing her sounded like a great idea, he would never push Abby into doing anything before she was ready.

"That sounds nice. It's been a long time since I spent a day doing nothing except lounging in the sun."

"I'll come by and pick you up around eleven? Maybe you might want to sleep in and enjoy a leisurely cup of coffee." Shane was considering how quiet the house would be for her. "Unless you want to come out sooner. Give it some thought; you can let me know later. I'm flexible."

"That sounds like heaven." Abby smiled. "The distraction will be good for me. To be honest, I'm worried about leaving Devin for the weekend. They've only had him for a few hours during the afternoon, and Tim grew up with an au pair. I don't know how they'll manage."

She gave an involuntary shiver, and he pulled her into his arms. "I'm sure I'm worried for nothing, but I'll be glad when this first visit is behind us."

Smoothing her hair, he held her close. "Before you know it, Monday will roll around, and you'll be headed back to Boston. If you want company, I make a good copilot," he released her.

"I'll give that some thought. But you're right; time will

fly. The Martin's have asked to see him every other month for an extended weekend. When I see them, I'm going to remind them they have an open invitation to come to Loudon. I have plenty of room."

She placed a hand on his cheek. "I'm grateful my weekend just got a little busier. Although Mr. and Mrs. Martin are his grandparents, I don't get a warm and fuzzy feeling from them."

"That's a good idea. If you make them feel they're welcome in your life, things may smooth out with them. But in the meantime..." Shane pulled her deeper into his arms and let his lips softly touch hers, tentative at first, waiting for her to lead him. At her response, the kiss deepened, causing sparks and fanning the flames. Before the fire started to roar, the baby's giggle could be heard on the monitor and it brought the flames to a smolder.

Shane paused mid-kiss and cocked his head. "I guess there's a little man who wants some of your attention, too." Reluctantly, he released her. After a last lingering kiss that was filled with longing and promise, they headed into the house.

Shane enjoyed a leisurely day with Abby and Devin. He played on the floor with the baby while she threw together a light dinner of salad and grilled fish. She kept an eye on them. "I'm thrilled with the way he has taken to you. Typically, he was shy around people, particularly men, but from the moment he laid eyes on you, he was hooked."

Abby looked away and finished plating dinner. During the meal, with the high chair between them, Devin soaked up their attention like a thirsty sponge. He squealed each time Shane took something from his plate and gave it to him.

When dinner was over, and the kitchen was tidy again, Shane didn't want the day to end, not just yet. "Abby, let's take Devin for ice cream. We can go to the park and watch the world go by in the sunset."

"Perfect way to top off a healthy dinner." She grinned. "I'll grab a light jacket for the baby." Abby tucked extra wipes and a sippy cup into the small diaper bag, then secured it over the stroller's handles.

Devin squealed the moment he saw the stroller. "This is one good reason to live on Main Street: a short walk to Scoops." Shane pushed the stroller down the sidewalk with Abby at his side, her hand resting lightly on one of the handles.

"I missed their ice cream when I lived out East. It adds ten pounds to your hips just looking at it, but it is heaven for your taste buds." Abby smacked her lips, causing Shane to laugh out loud and the neighbor's dog to bark.

"I'm the first one to say I love the stuff, but I think you've elevated it to a whole new level. Let's hurry. We don't want them to run out. I need to see what heaven tastes like," Shane joked.

"You jest; if you're not careful, I might just race you there, and the winner buys."

"It wouldn't be a fair race since I'm pushing the baby." Shane lengthened his stride.

Abby looked at him sideways. "You're going to use Devin as an excuse for coming in last? Typical." Batting her eyelashes, Abby tried to appear innocent in an attempt to cover the mirth that filled her eyes.

On their short ten-minute walk, she admired shop windows and overflowing flower boxes. When they reached Scoops, they saw the line was out to the sidewalk. "I think everyone in town had the same idea. Let's sit out here until it thins out." Abby pulled the stroller close to the bench while Devin played with a few toys.

Shane sat next to her, not quite touching. "I never thought to ask; can Devin eat ice cream?"

"He can have a little plain vanilla. It won't hurt him."

"Whew, I wasn't going to eat ice cream in front of him. I'd feel funny."

Abby laughed at him. "If we were going to have spicy Mexican food, which I'm not going to feed him, you're saying you wouldn't eat?"

"That's different. Ice cream is a treat. That's all I was thinking." Shane was annoyed that she was still snickering. "Do you need to keep laughing?"

"I'm sorry." She wiped tears away from her eyes. "I don't know why that struck me as so funny. I've checked with his pediatrician, and he said that at this age Devin can eat most everything, but to stay away from peanuts and spicy foods until he's older." Abby attempted to soothe Shane's ruffled feathers. "It's okay; I had the same concerns."

She glanced into the shop. "Look, we can go in."

Shane tickled Devin's cheek. "Don't worry, little man; I got you covered. Guys always stick together."

She studied the contents in the freezer case while Shane observed her contemplating the perfect choice. After careful deliberation, she smiled at the teenage girl behind the counter who was waiting patiently for her order.

"Abby, you can choose more than one flavor," said Shane.

She glanced at him out of the corner of her eye. "I didn't know you were in a hurry." She laughed. "I'm ready."

"I would like two scoops of butter pecan on a sugar cone with chocolate sprinkles," she announced.

Shane looked at her. "Didn't you forget something?"

"No, I don't think so. I really like butter pecan and sprinkles. I always have it as my first cone of the season."

"Devin? Are you going to order his or does he have to do it?" Shane teased.

"Oh, gosh. Also, I need a kid-sized scoop of vanilla, in a dish, please."

*A*bby squatted next to Devin. "Sorry, little one. Auntie got overwhelmed. There are too many choices, and they all look yummy!"

Devin, full of smiles, jabbered away without a single care. Shane watched the two of them, and their bond was evident. He understood why Kelly and Tim had chosen her as his guardian.

Shane ordered a triple scoop strawberry cone. Passing his cone to Abby, she gasped, "This is going to melt before you finish it."

He maneuvered the stroller out of the shop as Abby held the door open with her backside.

"Can you juggle everything for a couple of minutes? I'd like to sit in the park."

Abby placed Devin's cup on the stroller's canopy and carefully balanced the extra-large cone of strawberry while licking drips of butter pecan.

"You read my mind, but we should put a wiggle on it before I end up wearing more than you'll eat."

Devin was finishing the last of his ice cream, tilting the cup upside down, when Ray and Cari crossed the grass hand in hand. They came over to chat with Shane and Abby.

Cari bent over to peck cheeks and then diverted her attention to Devin. Ray shook hands with Shane and hugged Abby. "Hi, kids. How was your ice cream? Devin seems to be wearing an appropriate amount."

"May I?" Oblivious to the sticky mess, Cari unbuckled Devin from his seat. "Enjoy your cones," she said happily.

"Mom, why are you in town? I thought you'd be at Jake's."

"We just came from there. Sara was talking about baking muffins or something for her parents. I thought it would be easier for her if we got some things from the shop and dropped them off. Despite the fact they came to help her, she's still trying to be the good hostess and is running herself ragged."

Ray laughed. "No one expects Sara to do anything except be a new mommy and recover from her surgery. So, what are you guys up to tonight, besides having ice cream running down Shane's arms?"

He shrugged. Using a paper napkin, he hastily wiped it off. He had been too busy watching his mother cuddle Devin to notice his cone. "We finished dinner and decided it was a nice night for a walk and a treat. It's pretty handy living in town and close to Scoops. Also, I'm attempting to keep Abby from worrying. Devin's going to visit his grandparents for the weekend, and she's missing him already." Sliding his arm around her shoulders, he gave her a reassuring squeeze.

"What are you worried about?" Cari quizzed.

"Kelly had never left Devin overnight with her in-laws. Tim was raised by an au pair, and I don't know if they're ready to change diapers and be up at night if he's fussy," she explained. "I offered to stay for this first weekend, but they politely declined."

"Well, I'm sure there's nothing to worry about, and besides, it's only for two nights. You're picking him up on Monday morning?" Cari asked.

"I'm sure you're right; I'm being silly. Shane offered to go with me to pick him up, so I'll have backup in case the Martin's are difficult." Abby shrugged, dismissing her heavy heart.

"I thought I'd ask Don if he'll cover for me on Monday."

Ray and Cari attempted to hide their surprise. "That's a good idea. It's a lot of driving for one day, and I'm sure Abby will be happy for the company," Cari agreed, then turned to Ray. "Love, what do you say we let them finish their ice cream, and I can see there is at least one young man who will need to get hosed down when he's done." Laughing, she turned to Abby. "And I don't mean Devin."

Ray and Cari waved to the kids and then headed to the shop.

"I get the feeling we're going to be seeing more of Abby and the baby," said Cari.

Ray clasped Cari's hand. "Dear, I think you're right. It's about time, too."

Abby heard what they said but when their laughter drifted across the park to Shane and Abby he asked, "Now, what do you suppose those two are laughing about?"

Abby smiled. "We'll never know for sure, but if I had to guess, it had something to do with us."

10

Abby peeked through the billowing white curtains to confirm the weatherman's prediction. It was going to be a beautiful day. As an added bonus, she was spending it lakeside with Shane. Taking Devin to his grandparents had gone smoother than expected. The Martin's were thrilled to see him and had actually been friendly to her. She wasn't going to look a gift horse in the mouth. For the first time, Abby felt Devin would grow up surrounded by family.

Glancing at the time, Abby quickly dressed. She was running late. She packed a cooler with lunch and added marinated chicken and veggies for supper. She assumed Shane had a grill at his place.

At precisely eleven o'clock, she heard Shane's truck in front of her house. She peeked through the curtains as he jumped out and jogged up the front walk and around to the back door. She hurried into the kitchen and propped the door open with a jumbo-sized cooler. Then she rushed into the half bathroom to finish getting ready.

"Hello," he hollered into the darkened kitchen.

"Be right there!" Abby yelled from down the hallway.

Shane's smile lit up his face when he saw her pulling her hair into a stubby ponytail. Then she tucked it through the back of a pink baseball hat as she walked in the room. "You look great." He took in her short sundress and makeup free face. "You look like you did back in high school."

She grinned. "Hi there, handsome. Thank you for the compliment. Are you ready for some fun in the sun?"

"I've been looking forward to it, but what's in the cooler?" Shane quizzed.

"Well, you're providing the location and sun, so I'll provide the food and drinks. I hope you like what I've packed. I wasn't sure, so there's a little bit of everything." She was excited to have nothing to do but have fun and relax.

Shane grabbed the cooler's handles. Grunting, he hoisted it up. "What do you have in here, the entire contents of your refrigerator?" He pretended to struggle with it as he stepped out onto the back steps.

"You poor big strong man, do you want me to carry it for you?" she said in jest. "I may have gone overboard, but you won't be able to say you went hungry today. And if you do, it's your own fault."

Abby was perplexed as she watched Shane carry the cooler down the driveway. "You know it has wheels, right?"

Shane quickly covered his flub. "Of course, I was trying to impress you with my muscles."

She hid her laughter under a cough and followed him.

With the cooler stowed in the flatbed, he looked through his dark glasses and asked, "Ready?"

She nodded. "Let's go be lazy."

Abby hadn't been to the lake in years. He said he had bought a lakefront cottage, and that renovations had been going forward for several years. She was awestruck when he parked the truck in the driveway.

"You did buy the old McIntyre place. Jeez, I think the last time we were out here it was after the junior prom. Remember the beach party? This house was falling apart; windows were broken, and the porch was a death trap. But I remember the path to the beach area was mowed."

"Old man McIntyre was still alive then." Shane guided Abby to the back while she drank in the view.

"You've transformed the place; the flower gardens and wraparound porch are beautiful. I see you have your mother's green thumb. Clearly, you've done a lot of work."

Shane looked at his home as if seeing it through new eyes. "It had been a wreck when I bought it, but even as a kid, I loved this place. When Mr. McIntyre wasn't able to keep up outside, he hired me to take care of the grass. I never charged him; being at the lake was enough payment. I dreamed that someday I would wake up to the sounds of life on a lake. The hard work has been worth it. My home is my refuge."

"You've done a wonderful job, and I'm sure Mr. McIntyre would be happy to see how everything looks around here." Abby bent to smell a tiny rose bud.

"Thank you. You should bring Devin out. You'd have the place to yourself. I can picture Devin playing in the sand and splashing in the cool lake."

Once again, the famous McKenna generosity struck her. "That's sweet of you to offer. We might just do that."

On the sandy strip of beach, she spotted two lounge chairs and a table, close enough to enjoy the breeze off the water and on a slight incline to enjoy the spectacular view. It was peaceful. Abby witnessed the occasional fish jumping out of the water and the birds singing in the trees, a picture-perfect setting for the day ahead.

"Come on. I'll give you the nickel tour. We can leave the cooler on the porch." Shane opened the door and gestured for Abby to go ahead of him.

She stepped into an open floor plan; the kitchen, dining, and living room dominated two-thirds of the first floor. It was surrounded by glass that took advantage of the expansive view. Shane pointed and said, "Down there on the right is the master bedroom and a bathroom. There is also a half-bath off the kitchen with the laundry room, and upstairs there are a couple of bedrooms and a joint bath, but that isn't finished yet." Shane gestured up the stairs.

"Make yourself at home, mi casa, su casa." He grinned. "And that is all the Spanish I know."

"It's beautiful. You have a good eye. I should have realized your landscape designs would be impressive, too." Abby soaked in the details of the open space.

He pulled her hand. "Let's go outside; we're wasting sunshine hanging out in here." He seemed in a hurry to get back outside.

Abby flashed him a megawatt smile, then turned and walked out the sliding doors as she slipped her shades in place.

After they settled in the lounge chairs, Shane brought up the subject of Devin. "So how did it go yesterday with the Martin's?"

"Better than I expected. They were gracious and thrilled to see the baby. And they showed me a bedroom they had set up for him. I guess I had no reason to worry.

For the first time, I have hope that we can work together and give Devin the love and stability he deserves." Abby sighed, content in the warm sunshine.

"I broached the subject of the Martin's coming to Loudon for a visit. I explained I have plenty of room. You know, I think that surprised them." Abby sat up and looked at Shane. "You'll think I'm crazy, but I'll feel better after this weekend is over and I can pick him up and hold him in my arms. I'm being overprotective, but I can't help it."

Shane was quick to interject. "I disagree. You're taking the responsibility of being a parent seriously and doing what is best for Devin. You completely changed your life when Kelly died, and I have yet to hear one word of self-pity from your lips."

"It's been tough, but I didn't have a choice. Kelly and Tim trusted me to do what is right for their son, and I *will* do my very best to live up to their expectations. Even when his parents demanded that I relinquish custody, I knew I couldn't. Devin is the only family I have left, and we need each other." Abby quickly turned away from Shane as tears slipped down her face. If he saw them he didn't say a word.

"How about we get a quick dip in before lunch? This lounging works up a man's appetite." He offered his hand to Abby and pulled her to her feet. "Last one to the raft makes lunch!"

She threw her hat and sunglasses on the chair and took off at a dead run. There wasn't any chance she was coming in last. Taken by surprise, Shane took off after her. Abby shrieked as she flopped into the icy water, swimming hard toward the raft. It was a dead heat as they lifted themselves onto the hot boards.

"Jeez, when did you get competitive *and* fast?" He drew gulps of air into his lungs.

"I always was; you just didn't pay attention to your sister's scrawny friend." She laughed, her chest heaving with exertion.

"Maybe I should have, it might have made things more interesting."

He pushed himself to rest on his elbow. He could see the water droplets glistening on the tips of her eyelashes. He gently brushed the water from her face. His hand cupped her cheek as he lowered his lips to hers. His kiss deepened, and he edged closer. They didn't feel the rough planks that lay underneath them. Heat flooded Abby's body; the icy water quickly forgotten, her skin warmed under his touch. He melted into her; it was indistinguishable where she started and he left off. His kiss deepened. Their tongues dancing in a passionate expression of them coming together.

Abby had forgotten what it was like to be thoroughly kissed by a man, but she was sure it had never been this sensual. Her body responded as his hand caressed her arm, lightly sliding down her thigh. She groaned in pleasure as his touch set off a chain reaction of goose bumps followed the trail. A screech penetrated the fog that enveloped her brain. Abby pulled back to witness a hawk descending with talons extended, snatching lunch from the water. A nervous laugh escaped as she struggled to regain her composure.

He studied the woman that lay beneath him. "What's so amusing?" he asked in a low husky voice.

"The hawk, he's getting takeout for lunch. It made me realize I'm hungry, aren't you?"

"Not for food, but if you are, we can swim back."

She needed to regain control. She had kissed her share of guys, but no one had ever had this effect on her. She had felt the normal desire, heat, and need, but kissing Shane brought up feelings she couldn't put into words.

"I'm not racing this time. I won, and you're fixing lunch. Besides, a nice leisurely swim will cool us off." She looked at him, hoping the double meaning hit its mark.

He nodded. "Agreed," he said and pulled her up. "Ladies first."

She dove neatly into the water, creating a small ripple, with Shane close behind. They struck up an easy pace, side by side, as they swam back to shore. Abby stooped to towel off before unpacking the cooler.

He peered over her shoulder. "Did you think you were feeding my entire family?"

"I got a little carried away, but there is stuff for dinner too in case you're interested," she said shyly.

Quick to respond, Shane said, "I like the way you think."

He ate his way through a variety of containers, proclaiming each was the best he had ever had. She watched him, amused that he seemed to be a bottomless pit.

"Did you save room for a brownie?" she teased.

He looked up with twinkling eyes and patted his stomach. "I think there's room for one, maybe two."

She passed him a container. "Mr. McKenna, I think you're going to need a nap, and I doubt you're going to be hungry later for dinner."

"Don't worry; I always make room for a good meal." Shane took a large bite of the fudgy brownie. Rolling his eyes, he pleaded, "Don't tell my mother, but you make one helluva brownie."

$\mathcal{S}$unday dawned to another spectacular day. Abby relaxed on the front porch with a cup of coffee and a light breakfast. It was a treat to sit and watch the world go by. She was missing Devin but pushed the thought aside. Tomorrow, she would pick him up and be back in their routine. She grinned, enjoying the memory of yesterday—great company, good food and drinks, and a hot make-out session. When Shane brought her home, she had been tempted to ask him in, but based on the flames that were well fanned while they were kissing, she wasn't ready to leap into that fire.

The phone rang and interrupted her train of thought.

"Hello?"

"Hi, Abs. What are you up to today?" Kate's cheerfulness rang out.

Abby was pleased to hear Kate on the other end. "Hello, Kate. How are you?" She stretched her legs out in front of her.

"Great. My mom asked me to give you a call. We're all going over later to Mom's place for a cookout and thought you might want to join us. They'd love it if you could come by. Unless you've had your fill of the McKenna's."

Ignoring the past sentence, she asked, "What time is everyone getting together?" Abby hoped she had time to get her projects done.

"About three, I think. You don't need to bring anything, just yourself."

"Sounds good, see you later. And Kate?" Abby paused. "Thank you. It's a little too quiet at my house today."

Pleased with the change in her day, Abby hung up the phone. It was nice of Kate to call and invite her for a cookout. Maybe she would have the opportunity to talk with her. Something wasn't quite right with her old friend; there was a sadness that clouded her eyes. Whatever it was, she was sure that in time Kate would confide in her.

"*S*ee you soon, Abby." Kate disconnected and turned to look at her husband. "Once again, Mom nailed it. She was missing Devin."

*K*ate wriggled into her husband's arms and gave him a deep, scorching kiss. "We have a couple of hours. Can I interest you in a nap? You're looking a little worn out, and frankly, it would do us both a world of good." Kate's fingers toyed with a button on Don's shirt.

Sweeping his wife off her feet, he turned down the hallway. "Love, that's the best idea you've had today."

*E*llie's car was parked in the driveway when Abby arrived. She jumped off the back porch to greet her.

"Hi, Abby. What did you bring?"

"Pie. I couldn't show up empty-handed. When I was a kid, my mom drilled into me that you always take something with you when invited to a meal or party." Lifting up the tray, she said, "I'm sure it won't be as good as Kate's, but it's edible."

"We didn't invite you so you'd cook for our clan; it's your weekend to relax." Ellie took the basket as they walked to the house.

Cari greeted Abby warmly, "Hi, Abby. I couldn't help but overhear; I'm sure your pies will be better than what we make. Being in the baking business takes some of the pleasure out of eating dessert. But when someone else bakes, all I can say is 'move over!'" Cari looked her over with a sharp eye. "It looks like you got some sun yesterday. What did you think of Shane's house?"

"He's done a wonderful job with the old cottage. I almost didn't recognize the place. And we had a lot of fun. The water was cold, but it's only June. I had forgotten it takes until late summer for the water to really get warm."

She felt right at home back among the McKenna family. Growing up, she had spent many happy hours with Kate. It was a sharp reminder of a simpler time.

"Kate and Don should be here soon, and of course Shane's coming; he wouldn't miss a family cookout. Jake and Sara are bringing the babies over, but I'm not sure how long they're staying. Sara is still recovering. Secretly, I think she's looking for a change of scenery. Have you met Sara's parents, Vera and Keith?"

Abby shook her head no.

"They're coming too. So, there will be plenty of willing hands to take care of the little ones." Cari rattled off information.

Abby had forgotten how large the family had grown in a short time.

"I guess I should have made more pie!" Abby exclaimed.

Cari laughed. "Not to worry. We have plenty of food. If anyone leaves hungry, it's their own fault."

"Is there anything that I can help with? Put me to work." Abby glanced around, looking for something to occupy her hands.

"Not a thing. We can relax until everyone gets here and then it's all hands-on deck." Ellie smiled at Abby. "Let's go catch up. I'm the only family member who hasn't had you all to herself yet."

Abby thought it was sweet that everyone had welcomed her back with such warmth. She followed Ellie to the Adirondack chairs overlooking the flower garden. Ellie handed her a glass of iced tea.

"So, I hear you're dating my brother." Ellie studied her from behind huge sunglasses.

Direct and to the point. She couldn't fault Ellie for beating around the bush. "Yeah, I guess I am. We've gone out, which you knew, and yesterday we spent some time at the lake. He's a nice guy, one of the nicest I've met in a long time." Abby reclined in the chair with her eyes closed. "Ellie, can I ask you something, and please tell the truth. What's the family scuttlebutt? Does anyone object?"

"Everyone thinks it's great. You're the first girl that Mom has known about in years. Usually, Shane doesn't bring girls home. An interesting tidbit for you: Once Shane knew you were coming today, he said 'yes' before Mom could ask him if he'd like to come out. So, we figure he is really interested in you." Ellie wondered how Abby would take this information.

A smile hovered on Abby's lips. She liked the sound of Shane being smitten.

"You think he likes me."

"Yeah, definitely. Rumor has it he's attached to your nephew and the feeling is mutual." Ellie let that comment hang in the air.

Abby and Ellie sat in companionable silence while Abby tried to figure out how to respond.

"I'm pretty smitten with him, too," she said softly.

Ellie held her tongue and smiled. Before she could dig for details, Cari called out to them.

"Girls, Jake and Sara are here. Would you mind helping them lug baby paraphernalia into the house?"

"Sure." They jumped up to follow Cari.

Sara eased out of the car. As the girls approached, she waved.

Abby hoped she'd get a chance to hold at least one of the babies. She had wonderful memories of cuddling Devin as a newborn.

Abby hugged Sara. "Congratulations, Mommy. What can I take?"

Sara looked around and laughed. "Anything you can carry." Jake was unloading the back of the van, and a mountain of stuff was piling up next to the driveway. Abby grabbed two overstuffed bags and waited to see if any more help was needed.

Sara unbuckled Kaylee and passed her to Ellie, who carefully tucked her into a stroller. Sara then secured the boys in a double-wide version. She was surprised the process was going so smoothly. "Ellie, would you take Kaylee into the backyard while I get the boys?"

Ray came around from the side yard. "Hi, kids!" he called out. "Is there anything left that needs to go out back?" Taking note of the porta cribs and the other items sitting on the grass, he said, "We should get some of these items for our house. I don't want it to be hassle for you two to bring my grandchildren over." Ray grinned. "I always dreamed of a large family. Now we have three grandchildren, all at the same time." He clapped a hand on Jake's shoulder. "Well done." He picked up two porta-crib bags and headed towards the house.

Sara's parents, Keith and Vera Decker, pulled in behind the kids and quickly got their car unloaded while Cari lent a hand. It didn't take long until everyone was relaxing.

*S*hane got out of his truck. Damn, everyone seemed to already be here. Including Abby. He could see the porta cribs inside the sunroom but within earshot. Abby's eyes locked with Shane's just as he looked in her direction. The conversations and people blurred as he made his way to her side and bent down for a discreet kiss. "Hello," he whispered for her ears alone.

The family pretended they didn't notice the couple and kept the conversation humming. Talk continued to swirl with stories of the triplets until it turned to Abby's nephew, Devin.

"Abby, I'm sorry we didn't get to meet Devin today. Sara told me he's a cutie," Vera said. "Keith and I were very sorry to hear about your sister and her husband's accident. You're doing an admirable job, taking on the responsibility of raising him as a single parent. It takes a special person to turn their life upside down and put Devin's needs first."

"I'm sorry he's not here too. He's with his grandparents in Boston. Shane and I are picking him up tomorrow, so hopefully, you'll get to meet him while you're in town. We usually walk to Cari's shop in the early afternoon. He loves Cari and has become a flirt with all the ladies. We were lucky. My parents kept our childhood home, so it made the decision to move back easy. I didn't want to raise Devin in the city. Now, I need to find a job where I can make a living and still be able to take care of the baby." She glanced at the floor, feeling uncomfortable that she had monopolized the conversation and that she mentioned needing a job.

Cari jabbed her son in the ribs and gave a slight nod in Abby's direction.

"Ah, Abs, it just so happens I'm looking for an office manager, and I've been procrastinating. The office is in my house, but if you were interested, well, you wouldn't have to worry about daycare until you wanted to. I could set up a play area for Devin and maybe put a crib in the spare room upstairs." Shane stumbled over the offer.

Surprised, Abby looked at Shane. "You want to hire me to run your office? I don't know anything about the landscape business. I worked in a law firm."

Kate interjected, "I think it's a great idea, at least until you find something else. It will help you both. Abby knows computers and accounting, and she can handle a phone. How hard can Shane's business be? This will be a cinch. The way I see it, this is a win-win."

Shane nodded in agreement. "If it turns out it's not a good fit for either of us, at least it will give you time to look for something else. I can pay a fair salary, and you can have somewhat flexible hours." Shane didn't want to beg, but he thought this was a great idea, the bonus being that he would get to see Abby on a daily basis.

She quickly considered the pros and cons. "I'll take it, but only if you think I'll do a good job and it's not because you feel sorry for me."

"It's not, so it's settled," Shane said with a smile. "I expect you and Devin at my house at nine o'clock Wednesday morning."

"Shane, I can start Tuesday. You're already giving me special treatment," Abby teased.

"No, not special treatment." He chuckled. "I have tomorrow off, and I'm going to need Tuesday to clean my office. My new office manager should be able to find the desktop."

Everyone chuckled because they knew what Shane said was true, yet an understatement at the same time.

Abby marveled at how her life had changed since moving to Loudon. She didn't think it could get any better than it was right then because, at that moment, it was almost perfect.

12

Abby expertly maneuvered the SUV through the streets on the north side of Boston to the suburb of Hamilton. Shane happily rode shotgun. Her excitement bubbled over as she navigated up a long drive with a perfectly manicured lawn on each side and then stopped in front of an impressive house that oozed money.

Looking at Abby, Shane said, "This is where Tim grew up?"

"Maybe now you understand a little better why his parents weren't happy when he married Kelly."

He nodded. This house also explained why Abby was wary of these people.

With the car parked, she ran up the front steps and rang the doorbell. After several minutes, a woman she didn't recognize opened the door.

"Hello, I'm Abby Stevens. Is Mr. or Mrs. Martin available? "

"I'm sorry, Miss Stevens. Mr. and Mrs. Martin have gone away on an extended vacation."

Abby stared at her slack jawed. Shocked, she stammered, "I'm sure there must be some misunderstanding. I'm here to pick up Devin. They're expecting me. If you would let me come inside for a moment, I'm sure we can get this cleared up."

"No, I don't think so, Miss Stevens. They left Saturday. However, they asked me to give you this." The woman produced an envelope from her pocket. "Now, please excuse me." She firmly closed the door in Abby's face.

She turned to Shane. "What is this, some kind of cruel joke?"

He steered Abby back to her car. "Let's read the letter and go from there."

Abby leaned against the car. "Read it," she croaked, her voice thick with tears, and handed the letter to Shane.

He unfolded the letter, glanced at the contents, and then at Abby.

Abigail-

We appreciate all that you've done for Devin, our son's only child. However, after giving it careful consideration, we feel it is in his best interest that we have full custody. We can provide him every advantage that you're not equipped to do. This will also allow you to have the life that you deserve, as a young woman unencumbered by a small child. Of course, we will allow you to have supervised visitation with him in the coming years. Our legal team will be in contact with you. You will need to sign the documents to sign your rights over to us. Please, don't worry about Devin; he is well and perfectly safe with us. We have gone away for an overdue family vacation.

Sincerely,

Edward and Louise Martin

Shane finished reading as Abby's sobs tore at his heart.

"I have to find him," she cried. "I tried to do the right

thing for Devin, and now the Martin's have taken him from me. I've let Kelly down."

He wrapped his arms around her until the tears subsided. "I'll drive." He helped her into the car and fastened her seatbelt. "We can't think straight sitting here." He dropped the vehicle into drive and pulled away from the house, driving aimlessly while Abby stared out the window in silence.

He found a fast food restaurant's parking lot. He glanced at her and pulled his cell from his pocket. He punched the speed dial number for What's Perkin' and waited. "Mom?"

"Shane, what's wrong?" said Cari. She had a sixth sense when it came to her family. He could tell she was in full alert mode the minute she heard his voice.

"We're fine, but when we got to the Martin's, we discovered his grandparents had taken off with Devin. They left a letter telling Abby they plan on raising Devin and they told her to sign over custody to them. They said their lawyers have the papers ready for her. She's is hysterical, and I don't know what to do next." Shane exhaled, feeling relieved to get it out.

"Thank heavens you're both safe. Son, are you driving?"

"No, we're sitting in a parking lot. I think we're about a mile from the Martin's house."

"Let me think."

He could picture Cari pacing behind the counter and he was sure Kate was standing in the kitchen doorway.

"Kate handed me a note. She asked if Abby has the number of the lawyer who handled Tim and Kelly's estate?"

Shane held tight to Abby's hand and asked, "Mom is

wondering if you have the number of Tim and Kelly's lawyer?" She nodded and handed her phone to Shane.

"Yes, she has it."

"Good. Tell her to call them and say it's an emergency. They'll know what she should do. In this situation, it's best to get her lawyer working on it immediately. One thing in her favor is that she didn't know the Martin's were going to take off with the baby. And she has legal custody, so they broke the law. I'm not sure how much trouble the Martin's will be in, but I'm confident that calling the lawyer is the best place to start."

Shane told his mother he would be in touch after they talked with the lawyer. He disconnected and took Abby's cold hands in his. Despite the heat, she was chilled to the bone.

"Abs. You have to call Tim's lawyer and tell him this is an emergency and you need an appointment today." He spoke quietly, not wanting to push but knowing speed was critical.

She sat frozen. She couldn't move. He released one hand and took her phone. He scrolled through the list of contacts.

"Is this it, Baird and Cohen?" Shane turned to show her the entry.

Her eyes were huge. She blinked in an attempt to focus and finally she slowly nodded.

Shane hit the CALL button. Someone answered on the second ring.

He introduced himself to the woman on the other end and rapidly explained what had happened. He inquired if there was any possibility Abby could talk with someone today. He waited on hold, impatient for the receptionist to check the appointment book.

"Mr. McKenna? I was able to reach Mr. Baird, and he said he would make time for Ms. Stevens at three. You may have to wait for a bit as he will be coming from court, but he will definitely see her today."

He thanked her and confirmed they would be there. He turned to Abby, giving her hand a reassuring squeeze. "We have an appointment this afternoon."

She sat in silence while the minutes passed by on the digital clock. Shane patiently waited, holding her hand until she was ready to talk.

"Why did they do this? Why did they take Devin from me? I'm not a bad person, and I love him with all my heart. Everything I do is for him. That's why we moved back to Loudon. I don't understand why."

"I don't think it has anything to do with you. I think they were probably ticked off because Tim and Kelly chose you over them. To Kelly and Tim, you were the only logical choice." He tried to comfort her but wasn't sure what else to say.

"Do you think we'll be able to bring Devin home today?" She looked at him with a glimmer of hope shining in her eyes.

He didn't think there was a chance of that, but he wasn't going to say anything to dash her hopes; hope was all she had at the moment.

"We'll know more after we talk to Mr. Baird. Do you know him?" Shane tried to shift the subject to something that would help Abby get through the next few hours.

"Yes, Kyle Baird was my lawyer when we appeared before the judge. He was a personal friend of Tim's. I'm sure he'll know what to do." Abby was beginning to feel better. Kyle had gotten her through those first few days after the funeral, and he would defend the wishes of his late clients.

"It's going to be a long day; let's get something to eat. We need to keep our energy up."

"I'm not hungry, but okay. I know the area." She thought for a minute and gave Shane directions to a local seafood restaurant. "It has good food, and it's close to Kyle's office."

He pulled out of the parking lot. She was withdrawn as he navigated through light traffic. He glanced at her several times, trying to gauge how she was holding up.

After ten minutes, she said, "It's on the left."

Shane pulled into the nearly vacant parking lot and parked under the small tree near the back. "Are you ready?"

Abby nodded and opened the door. "Sorry about the lack of conversation."

The couple walked to the entrance, and Shane opened it, allowing her to go in first.

"I guess fish is a specialty here." Shane smiled at her, wishing the circumstances were better for their lunch date. With the lunch rush over, they were seated within moments. Their table overlooked the water. It was beautiful, but the day had lost its luster. They glanced over the menu and placed their order.

She looked at her watch and then at Shane. "The next few hours are going to be torture."

He agreed with her but attempted to get her mind focused on something productive instead. "We should make a list that details how often you've had contact with the Martin's and include the positives about Loudon and your house. In some way, it may help the lawyer."

She retrieved a small notepad and a pen from her bag.

"This is a good idea and it will give me something to do while we wait."

She gave Shane a weak smile. "I recently got a job that is parent-friendly. A house, mortgage-free and in good repair. I've found an excellent pediatrician, and he can vouch that Devin is thriving. I don't know what else I can tell him. Oh, the final benefit, I have friends, a support system." Abby tapped the pen on her chin as she thought about the life she was building for Devin.

"How are you managing his trust fund?" Shane prodded. "I get the impression Tim's parents are motivated by money and power."

She jotted down the name of the investment company. She was very careful with her money and could justify, down to the penny if necessary, all expenses related to Devin's well-being. "I haven't touched his trust fund. There is an interest check each month, and I deposit it into a savings account. The Martin's can't say I'm stealing his money."

"Is there anything Tim's parents might try to use against you?" Shane wondered out loud.

"Well, I haven't had a date until you, so they can't say that I'm being promiscuous or exposing Devin to a revolving door of men. And nowhere did Tim and Kelly state that I needed to become an old spinster. But their letter did mention something about me living a single girl's life."

Abby was interrupted as their lunch was served. It smelled delicious. She reached for her fork as Shane reached across the table and placed his hand on hers.

"Abs, I'll be with you every step of the way, and I can speak for my family when I say they're here for you, too."

Tears filled Abby's stormy eyes. "That means more to me than you'll ever know. Thank you."

he office of Baird and Cohen was quiet when Abby and Shane arrived. The receptionist informed them Mr. Baird was running late; he was still in court. Disheartened, they settled on the stiff leather chairs to wait.

For the umpteenth time, Abby glanced at her watch. This waiting was driving her crazy. She glanced at Shane, who was leafing through a business magazine he'd found on a table. He appeared to be studying every word.

"Is that a good article?" The question came out sharper than she intended.

"Huh? I'm sorry, Abby. I've been staring at the same page, and I can't seem to concentrate. I'm baffled; if they wanted to challenge the custody arrangement, why not just take you to court?"

"It might have something to do with a letter that Tim left them. Kyle gave it to them at the reading. I never knew the contents. Mr. Martin slipped it into his coat pocket while Mrs. Martin glared at me. I don't remember much else; I'm sure I was numb. Tim and Kelly had appointed me Devin's guardian. I had been sure the baby would go to live with his grandparents. So, I can only imagine how they felt when Kyle announced I had full legal and physical custody."

The receptionist rose from behind her desk. "Ms. Stevens? Mr. Baird came in through the back entrance. He can see you now."

She led the way down a long quiet corridor into a bookcase-lined conference room. Kyle Baird sat at a polished black table with a thick folder in front of him. He looked up and crossed the room to them.

"Hello. Kyle Baird."

Shane took Kyle's extended hand and gave it a firm shake.

"Shane McKenna. I'm a friend of Abby's from Loudon."

"Abby, I'm sorry we have to meet under these circumstances." He shook her hand in a solemn greeting. "Please, sit down."

She sat at one end. She glanced at the neatly stacked pile of folders, and the top file had her name on the tab. The pain hit her like a rogue wave again as she realized she had a fight on her hands, and Kyle was preparing to rescue her and Devin.

He offered them each a bottle of water. He cleared his throat and withdrew a yellow legal pad from his briefcase.

Kyle paused, pen in hand, prepared to take copious notes. "Abby, I want you to tell me what happened when you got to the Martin's house, but let's start at the beginning. When did you take Devin to see his grandparents, and what arrangement did the three of you agree to?"

"As you know, part of the original agreement with them

was that Devin would spend one weekend every other month with his paternal grandparents. I call them every week with updates, and I e-mail pictures regularly. Finally, we agreed this would be the first visit. On Friday, I drove Devin to Boston, and I dropped him off with the understanding that I would come back midday today and pick him up. They never said anything about going away for the weekend. I was shocked when I arrived, and a stranger answered the door and gave me this letter." She withdrew the letter from her bag and slid it across the expanse of the table.

Kyle scanned the contents. Laying it to one side, he said, "Have you been arguing with them or denying access to the baby?"

"No," Abby wailed. "We've been getting along much better in the last couple of months. I've wanted them to spend time with Devin and they seemed to be supportive of our move to Loudon. I keep in contact with them regularly. This was the first time they said they wanted him to spend the weekend with them." Abby shrugged her shoulders, looking lost. "Kyle, you witnessed their reaction when they found out Tim and Kelly gave me custody. You know Mr. Martin was furious that Tim hadn't confided in him. Do you think they could have been planning to take Devin the first chance they got?"

"I can't say for sure, but they haven't helped their case in family court. Taking him away from his legal guardian and leaving a note adds support to our case. Bottom line: They kidnapped him."

Abby was stunned; she hadn't thought of Devin as having been kidnapped.

"This letter clearly states they don't plan to honor Tim and Kelly's wishes and what the court has deemed appropriate for the minor child. I can assure you this isn't going to make the judge happy."

"Will I get him back tonight?"

"Unfortunately, first we have to find them and request through the courts that they be ordered to return. I need to call the lawyer they used for the hearing. I'll do everything I can, but I have to be honest, this is going to take some time." Kyle looked from Abby to Shane. "Will you stay in the city tonight?"

Shane piped up. "That's not a problem; we'll stay, whatever it takes." He laid a comforting hand on Abby's arm.

She clung to his hand. "Don't you have to get back home? What about work?"

"Don't worry; Don will cover for me. I'm not going anywhere without you and Devin."

The tears Abby had been holding back slid unchecked down her cheeks. Kyle waited, giving her a moment to compose herself. "Abby, we need to go over a few things." He handed her a box of tissues.

She wiped away her tears and straightened her shoulders, "Of course, I'll tell you whatever I can."

During the next hour, Abby and Kyle went over finances, housing, friends, and the baby's health. Kyle excused himself from the room to make some calls.

Abby and Shane were feeling more confident than when they had arrived.

"I'm sorry I dragged you into this mess."

"Stop. I'm glad I was here. I don't want to think about you going through this alone, without the support of your friends. Was it this bad with the Martin's when you were formalizing custody?"

"Yeah. Kyle asked lots of questions about whether I

was willing to take on the responsibility, change my life, and basically raise Devin as my son. Of course, I agreed without hesitation." Abby crossed to the window and stared out into the late afternoon sun. "If the Martin's were concerned about anything, I wish they had talked to me instead of taking Devin and gone into hiding."

Kyle walked in and sat down. With a slight smile, he said, "I just got off the phone with Edward Martin's attorney and strongly suggested his clients get back to town and call as soon as they park their car. Otherwise, I will be filing a formal complaint at nine tomorrow morning and have them charged with kidnapping. An Amber Alert will be issued, and the Martin's will be arrested. The police will take it very seriously. I'll request a hearing as soon as I can get us before a judge. You won't have Devin back tonight, but I'm hopeful that by tomorrow at this time you'll be on your way home."

"And then what? Do I need to worry every time they have him for a weekend? Maybe the next time they'll leave the country!" Abby's voice shrilled. She desperately needed reassurance from Kyle.

"Abby, we'll have to go back to court and defend the custody arrangement. I'm sure they are going to sling a lot of mud in your direction. Social Services will get involved, and there will be home visits, both planned and unannounced, for you and the Martin's. I don't want to alarm you, but you need to be prepared." He gave her a reassuring look. "I have no reason to believe the custody arrangement will be overturned. However, until things are settled, I'll petition the court to have the Martin's visits supervised. I hope the judge will press the kidnapping angle, pointing out that what they did is a crime, punishable with jail time. I think that if it comes to their good name being dragged through the courts, the Martin's will play by the rules." He looked from her to Shane. "It's my guess they thought you wouldn't fight them, hoping you had grown tired of being a single parent to their grandson. But the courts will weigh heavily on the side of Tim and Kelly's written request."

Abby nodded as Kyle laid everything out. She could wait one night to see her sweet boy. She would do whatever it took to get him back.

Kyle stood up. "One last thing: Tim thought someday his parents might challenge custody so he set up an account for all legal expenses to be covered. I'll call you later and give you updates. Go, have some dinner, get a hotel room and settle in for the night. Okay?"

Shane shook hands with Kyle. "Thank you for fitting us in. We'll be close by." He passed him a slip of paper. "This is my cell number, in case something happens, and you can't reach Abby."

Kyle placed the number inside the folder. "Can you be here tomorrow morning at seven-thirty? Hopefully, at that time, we can make plans for you to pick up Devin. Abby, I'm afraid you're going to be making this drive a few more times before it's over with."

Abby narrowed her eyes and stood ramrod straight. "That won't be a problem; we'll be here. Thank you, Kyle."

She slowly walked out into the afternoon sun with Shane holding tightly to her hand. She had a heavy heart, wondering where her little guy was at that moment. She prayed the distance between them was shrinking with each minute that passed.

"Let's find a hotel room and then a drugstore. We should pick up a few things we'll need." He guided her to the car.

"It's going to be a very long night," she said softly. "Can we find a hotel close by in case we get a call, and I can pick Devin up tonight?"

"We passed a national chain down the road; it should be pretty good. Do you want to share a room, or do you want one to yourself? I promise I'll be a perfect gentleman." Shane gave her a sheepish grin.

For the first time since the nightmare began, Abby felt a genuine smile reach her lips.

"I'm going to hold you to that, McKenna. Don't make me call Cari and tell her your manners got lost somewhere between Boston and Loudon." She wagged a finger at him.

"Never!" He gave her a mock bow. "Miss, you have nothing to fear. My momma raised me right."

Abby's heart felt lighter as they checked into the hotel room. She was grateful Shane was with her.

After a quick stop at the store, he announced, "I'm going to check in with my mom. Why don't we go sit by the pool, have a cool drink, and when I'm done, we'll have an early dinner? Tomorrow is going to be a long day, and a good night's sleep will do us both some good."

Emotionally drained, Abby would have agreed to just about anything at that moment and sitting in the sun sounded relaxing. They stopped in the bar on the way outside and ordered two Cokes.

Kate answered Cari's house phone on the first ring.

"Shane, what's going on? Where is Devin?" Kate peppered him with questions before he could utter more than "hello."

"Sis, hold on. Get Mom and Ray and put me on speakerphone. That way I'll only have to tell the story once."

"Okay, hold on."

Shane could hear Kate yelling. After a brief pause, he heard a click, and the sounds of people gathered around the speaker.

Speaking softly, Cari said, "Shane, Abby, we're all here."

Shane put his cell on speaker and set it on the table.

"Hi, Mom. We can hear you."

"Here's the nutshell version. The Martin's took Devin and left town. They made the decision to release Abby from the responsibility for Devin without discussing it with her. But we've met with Abby's lawyer, who in turn called their lawyer and demanded they get back to town or charges would be filed against them for kidnapping." Shane paused and drew a deep breath.

Ray interjected, "Where are you now?"

"We've checked into a hotel about two miles from the Martin's home in case we can pick him up tonight, which is doubtful, but it helps us feel better knowing we can get there quickly."

She smiled at Shane. "Cari, Shane has been amazing. I don't know what I would have done without him." She took his hand.

"Abby, do you want us to come out tomorrow?" Cari asked. "We can pack a bag and be there; just say the word."

"No, you don't need to come out here. We're hoping to be back home sometime tomorrow with Devin. I'm not leaving without him."

"Of course, you're not. So, what can we do to help?" Ellie chimed in.

"At this point, all we can do is wait and hope this nightmare is over quickly. But I'll have to fight for him." Abby steeled herself at the thought of what was to come.

"We'll call tomorrow after we see my lawyer. We have an early appointment with him."

Shane said, "Kate, ask Don to handle things for me until we get back? There are a lot of jobs starting this week, but I can't let Abby face these people alone."

"Absolutely! We'll take care of everything until all three of you are home where you belong." Kate spoke for the family, not just her husband.

"Alright, we're going to let you go, and we'll call the shop tomorrow. Mom, can you call Jake and Sara, please?"

"Consider it done. We love you both, and Abby, sweetheart?" Cari waited until Abby answered her.

"I'm here," she said, her voice thick with tears.

"We love you and Devin. Keep these words close in your heart and draw strength from them over the next twenty-four hours. We'll see you soon."

"Thanks, Mom. That means a lot to both of us." Shane spoke for Abby, who was at a loss for words.

"Talk to you guys tomorrow, bye." Shane hung up, ending the conversation quickly.

He pulled Abby from the chair and into his arms, holding her while she wept. He gently smoothed her hair with his large calloused hands, waiting for the torrent of tears to run their course.

Exhausted, Abby looked at him through wet eyelashes and kissed him tenderly.

"I'm a mess, but I am so thankful you're here."

Shane returned her tender kiss. For now, it was enough to hold her in his arms. He said, "There isn't anywhere else I would rather be."

14

The alarm clock went off like a foghorn. Abby rolled over and slapped at the nightstand in an attempt to silence the noise. She had watched the numbers slowly roll by while wrapped in the security of Shane's arms. After a low-key dinner, they had come back to the hotel and turned on the TV, which was when Shane promptly fell asleep. Abby had spent the night willing the phone to ring with news. She couldn't remember ever having spent a more difficult night filled with worry and fear of the unknown.

Her only recurring thought was that she had let Kelly down. Kelly and Tim had trusted her to protect Devin from the world, and now the Martin's might be successful in taking him away. Abby thought about the three people she had lost over the last couple of years. If the court took Devin away from her, at least he was alive and would be well taken care of, even if it wasn't by her. After her mom had been diagnosed with stage four cancer, Kelly and Abby had spent every free moment with her, storing up a lifetime of memories in a few short months. When her mother passed away, she was at peace, comforted to know the girls had each other to lean on in the days and weeks ahead.

Shane stirred and rolled over. His eyes popped open. "Was that the phone?" He bolted out of bed and dashed into the bathroom. "Give me a minute and I'll be ready to go."

She gathered a few toiletries from the dresser. By the time Shane was finished, she was ready to take her turn.

She put a hand on his chest. "Relax, it's still early. We have time for breakfast before we meet Kyle," Abby moved to the bathroom doorway.

Before she could close the bathroom door, Shane put his hand out and stopped her. He gently tugged her hand. "Come here."

Drawing her tight to his chest, he kissed the top of her head. She melted into his arms. Time seemed to stand still as she prayed she would find the strength to get through the next few hours. When she eventually pulled back and looked up into his sapphire eyes, she could see dark circles smudged under them. Sleep had eluded him and she could only guess her eyes wore a similar look.

"I can see you didn't sleep much last night either. I'll drive today; maybe you can try and relax."

"I'll drive. You're the one who needs to chill."

"Shane, I won't relax or be going home until I have Devin safely in my arms," she said firmly.

"Abby, the lawyers involved will handle the Martin's. Devin will be going home with us. Now, go get ready. I'll get us checked out." He gave her a nudge toward the bath.

*K*yle was waiting for Shane and Abby in the conference room. The couple had a sense of déjà vu as the same receptionist escorted them down the hall. Kyle stopped typing as they entered the room. He stood up to shake hands with Abby and Shane.

"Good morning. I trust you slept a bit." Kyle looked at Shane, and his gaze slid to Abby. If he noticed the shadows under her eyes he didn't say anything. He gestured for them to sit and offered coffee before giving them the update.

Shane was thankful he had something to do with his hands. He watched Abby toy with her mug while they waited for Kyle to finish scanning the papers in front of him.

"Well, the good news is Edward and Louise Martin returned home late last night." He raised his hand as Abby started to interrupt him. "Hold on, Abby. I know what you're about to say."

Her body was taught like a piano wire, waiting to be sprung.

He slowly looked from Abby to Kyle. "Why didn't you call us? We could have picked him up last night," Shane demanded. "Are you working for Abby or Edward Martin?"

"Shane, let me reassure you, I work for Abby and Devin. I understand your frustration, but we need to show Abby is a caring, compassionate guardian, and one willing to put the child's best interest first. He was not in danger and letting him sleep at his grandparents' house was perfectly reasonable. Even given these circumstances. We can't give in to their irrational thinking. However, I did take some precautions. For instance, the house was kept under surveillance. I didn't think they would violate a court order, but I wasn't going to take the chance."

She nodded slowly. "I understand your logic, but it would have been helpful if you had called to let me know they were back."

"Abby, I was hoping you were getting some sleep. Be honest for a minute, would it have made a difference in how you spent your night, or would you have wanted to charge over there no matter the hour and demand to take him?" Kyle waited, giving her time. "Think about it. You were understandably distraught, and your first instinct would have been to go and get him. Am I right?"

Abby gave Kyle a hard look. She slammed the table top with her hand. "Of course, I would have wanted to pick him up. They tried to take him away from me!"

"Abby," Kyle implored. "We have to be smarter. We can use your restraint to our advantage when we go before the judge." He glanced at his watch. "Which we do at ten. In the meantime, we need to go over a few things."

He rearranged a few papers and she could see a copy of a letter resting on a legal pad.

"Abby, I need you to trust me just as Kelly and Tim did. The next couple of questions may make you even madder at me, but I need for you to be brutally honest. The Martin's may say that you indicated taking care of the baby has been too much for you and you've been anxious for Devin to visit his grandparents, so you could have some freedom. How would you respond to that?"

"That's insane! I wanted him to see his grandparents; they're family, and family is the only thing that truly matters in life. Everything I've done since my sister died is in his best interest. I left my job and moved to my family's home in a wonderful small town." Abby's hands were flying as she spoke. "I have baby-proofed it, found an excellent pediatrician, and reconnected with old friends. I have a support system in Loudon. I have been offered a job as an office manager, and I can take him to work with me. The office is in a house where I will have a bedroom set up for him and a play area. Honestly, I don't know what else I could do." Pausing, Abby shook her head and then continued, "I've never been a party girl, gone clubbing, or taken singles' vacations. I'm an average girl who has been charged with raising her sister's only child. A responsibility I take very seriously!"

Kyle nodded, jotting down notes as she talked. "How did you find the job that gives you the freedom to take Devin with you?"

Shane looked at Abby and jumped in the conversation. "Me. I own a landscaping company. I hire people I know and trust, mostly family and close friends. Abby has been a friend since childhood. She was at a family gathering and mentioned in conversation that she was looking for a job. I offered her the position. I was raised to believe that we take care of our friends and family, and I trust her to handle my business. "

Abby smiled as he spoke. "You can see I have a good support system in Loudon."

Kyle nodded again and added to his notes. "Now, what about the baby's trust fund? Have you used it for anything other than expenses related explicitly to Devin?"

"I haven't touched any money in the trust. I can handle our relatively low living expenses. I own the house outright, and it's in good repair. I have savings, which I've been using until I found this job. My intention for the trust fund is that it will be for college and for his future. Until then, I'll support him."

Kyle nodded, pleased with her response. "Will you be able to produce financial records for the court to review, if asked?"

"Certainly, if you think we need them today, I will call my bank and request the records to be faxed over to you." Abby looked at him expectantly, her cell phone was at the ready.

"I don't believe it will be necessary today, but I'm sure in the coming weeks the subject will come up."

"So, what should I expect today?" She wondered out loud.

"I'll explain the events as they have occurred since Friday to the judge. I will present a copy of the letter for the judge to review. I'm sure she'll ask a few questions. I'm confident the Martin's will be told to return Devin to your custody immediately. We will need to go back to court in a few weeks." Kyle summarized the process in an efficient manner.

"Will I be able to take him home to Loudon?" Abby stared at Kyle.

"Yes, I'm sure you'll be able to leave the city. Then our work will begin. Unless the Martin's give up their request for custody, you can expect home visits from a caseworker, your finances to be scrutinized, and the people you're close with to be interviewed. Hopefully, in a few months, this will be behind you and Devin."

"What about the Martin's? Do you think I'll have to worry about them taking off with him again? I can't live my life always wondering if he will be there when I go to pick him up after a long weekend."

"I expect when this is over you shouldn't have to

worry again. I'm hoping the Martin's get the fear of God in them today from the judge. For now, they'll fight for custody, but they won't step outside the law. Also, they too will be subjected to all the same things you'll be going through: home visits, financial review and interviews. They'll be concerned about their reputation in their social circle."

"I hope you're right, for everyone's sake," Shane's voice was flat.

"So, who will be at the hearing today besides the three of us?" Abby questioned.

"Edward and Louise Martin, their attorney, Judge Roy, a stenographer, and us."

"Where's Devin?" Abby looked at Shane, worry creeping over her face.

"The Martin's hired a nanny. They have been instructed to bring Devin with them today. So, I'm expecting the nanny to be waiting in the judge's chambers with Devin. After court, they shouldn't give you any trouble, but I will be with you and Shane," Kyle reassured them.

Abby glanced at her watch and saw it was almost nine. "Kyle, if we're all set, we need to go shopping for appropriate clothes for court. Right now, we're not exactly dressed to impress and I don't want that held against me."

Kyle glanced at their shorts and T-shirts. "That's not a bad idea. They expect you to show up looking like a teenager or the party girl they intend to conjure up. The right clothes will show the judge you're a mature adult. Go to Simon's Clothing. They open at nine and are two blocks south from here. They'll have what you need. I'll meet you on the courthouse steps, and we'll walk in together."

Abby and Shane thanked Kyle before they left the offices and made their way down the street. Abby spied the store first and steered Shane to the door. She quickly scanned the racks for a dress for herself and a pair of dark pants and a shirt for Shane.

Abby turned to the clerk. "Excuse me. Where is the dressing room?"

He pointed to the back corner and then refocused his attention on the newspaper he was reading, which took up the large expanse of the counter.

Not long after, Shane and Abby came out wearing their new outfits. "What do you think? Will we shock the Martin's?" Shane asked.

Abby nodded and stated, "I'm going to pay for your clothes."

Shane shook his head, "You're not buying my clothes. If spending a few bucks helps, then consider it done. I'm not going to do anything to jeopardize your custody of Devin. I'd wear a tuxedo if you asked me to!"

Abby chuckled. "Well, a tux won't be necessary, but I'm serious, I'm paying."

"Nope, you can pay me back by cooking me a fabulous dinner some night."

She looked at him with one eyebrow raised. "You really would be better off letting me pay. I don't cook like your mom."

Shane dismissed the comment with a pat on her backside. "We need to hustle. It's getting late."

They turned to the clerk and asked him for a pair of scissors. Abby proceeded to cut off the price tags. If the sales clerk thought it was odd, he never said a word while he rang up the sale.

Abby and Shane waited on the courthouse steps as

Kyle hurried over to them. He glanced at the new clothes, nodding in approval. "You guys clean up good," he remarked. "Are you ready?"

She steeled herself. "As ready as I can be."

To steady her nerves, she took a deep breath and placed her hand in Shane's as they walked into the hall of justice. Clearing security took several minutes. They emptied their pockets, and Abby's purse went through the scanner while the guard motioned for them to walk through the metal detector. After retrieving their personal items, Kyle escorted them down a long, brightly lit corridor lined with closed doors. He paused about halfway down, held open a dark stained wooden door, and ushered them inside.

A man in a uniform sat at the desk in the room.

"Hello. Kyle Baird, Abigail Stevens, and Shane McKenna to see Judge Roy," Kyle said to the officer.

Solemnly, the officer pointed to the inner door. "Go in. Judge Roy is expecting you."

The instant Abby entered, she saw Edward and Louise Martin, who were seated at a table with a man wearing an expensive looking suit. They turned and glared at her.

"Mr. Baird?" Judge Roy acknowledged the newcomers, gesturing the trio to come forward. "Please have a seat while I review the paperwork."

Minutes dragged as the judge scrutinized several pages, flipping back and forth between sections marked in the document. "It seems we have a problem." Judge Roy gave Edward a hard look.

"Yes, Your Honor," Kyle concurred.

The judge turned to study Kyle. "Mr. Baird, please tell me your version of the events leading up to today."

"My client, Ms. Stevens, took the minor child to visit

his paternal grandparents last Friday. Mr. and Mrs. Martin agreed that Abby would return to pick him up midday on Monday. When Ms. Stevens arrived, she found, to her shock, that the child wasn't there. She was handed a letter. I believe you have a copy of the letter." He gave a sharp look at Edward. "It instructed her to relinquish custody to Edward and Louise Martin." Kyle paused while the judge glanced at the letter.

"Mr. Martin, I assume you had a good reason for taking the child and leaving the state," Judge Roy stated, looking from Edward to Louise.

"Did you fear for the child's welfare?" she prodded them.

Edward Martin straightened his spine. "Your Honor, my wife and I believe that Ms. Stevens isn't fit to care for our grandson. We thought it best to release her from the burden of caring for Devin and give her the opportunity to live the life of an unencumbered young woman."

"Was this something Ms. Stevens indicated she wanted? And if you believed what you were doing was in the best interest of the minor child, why didn't you go through the proper channels to petition for a change in custody? Did you believe taking the child and leaving a note of explanation was the best course of action?" The judge took off her reading glasses and waited for a response. After a lengthy silence, the judge prodded Edward.

With a warning tone in her voice she said, "Mr. Martin, please remember you are addressing a judge, and it's not a wise idea to circumvent the truth."

Edward shrank back into his chair. "No, we did not have a conversation with Abigail; it was our decision based on what we felt our son should have done in the event of his untimely death. Instead, he and his wife chose Ms. Stevens to care for our grandson."

"I see. If I understand you correctly, it is your belief she is unfit to raise Devin Martin."

"There is money, Your Honor, a lot of money. She doesn't have any experience in handling a trust fund. We fear she will squander his inheritance." Edward glared at Abby with hard, black eyes.

Abby started to say something, but Kyle lightly touched her arm and shook his head, indicating she should wait.

"Ah, at the root of all evil, it's about money." Judge Roy turned to address Abby.

"Ms. Stevens. Do you wish to relinquish custody of the child?"

Holding herself still despite her nerves wreaking havoc on her insides, she said, "Absolutely not. My sister and brother-in-law entrusted their only child to my care. I will do whatever I must to care for and raise him into a fine young man, a person they would have been proud of."

Abby focused on Edward and Louise. "How could you do this? Go against their wishes?" she demanded.

"Our son should never have married your sister. If he hadn't, he'd still be alive today," Louise sniffed.

"Mrs. Martin, we are not here to discuss your son's choice of a spouse. We are discussing a little boy and his future." The judge reined in her temper. "Mrs. Martin, you and your husband will return the child to Ms. Stevens, who is free to return to her home in Loudon. Social Services will conduct several home visits in Loudon and at your home as well. Their job is to confirm what is in the best interest of the child, and I will be reviewing all the pertinent documents before I make my final decision. We will continue this hearing in three months. This should give the state sufficient time to conduct interviews and submit their report."

"What about the trust fund? She currently has unlimited access to a lot of money," Edward shouted. "I want to know that she isn't bleeding it dry!"

"Ms. Stevens, would you like to respond?" Judge Roy inquired, looking at Abby.

"Edward, not that it concerns you, but I haven't touched one penny of Devin's trust fund. I'm providing for us with my money. My intention for Devin is to satisfy his parent's wishes, attend college, and earn a degree. Based on the conditions of the will, some of the funds will be used to pay for his education. After graduation, he will receive another portion of money to start his life. Tim and Kelly set up the fund with a good financial group, and I'm confident it will continue to grow." Abby addressed the judge. "Your Honor, if necessary, I can provide a full accounting."

The judge suppressed a smile. "Will that suffice, Mr. Martin, Mrs. Martin?"

Edward gave a slight nod in agreement.

"Are there other concerns, Mr. Martin? Anything else we should clear up before I release the child into Ms. Stevens' care?"

"You're going to do what?" Edward demanded.

Louise clung to her husband's arm. "Do something!"

"Mr. Martin, you have given me no reason to reverse the original decision of this court. Ms. Stevens, from what I can tell, has done nothing to warrant the removal of the minor child from her home. Based on what your attorney submitted, the child is in excellent health and is thriving. Am I missing something?"

Red-faced, Edward slammed his clenched fist on the table. "We hired a nanny to take care of him, and she can certainly do a better job in the right kind of environment than Abigail can in Loudon."

Clearly annoyed, Judge Roy interrupted him. "Mr. Martin, a nanny and an elaborate nursery don't automatically guarantee you would be a better caregiver than Ms. Stevens. My decision is final; Ms. Stevens will be taking the child with her. And I caution you, if you make any attempt to take off with the child, I will have you arrested for contempt and put you and your wife in jail. Do I make myself perfectly clear?"

Seething, Edward looked at his lawyer. "What do I pay you for?"

Ignoring his client, Mr. Maynard addressed the judge. "Your Honor, the baby's things are at the Martin's home and will be ready for Ms. Stevens when she arrives." Mr. Maynard snapped his notebook closed. "And my clients will abide by your decision today. May I ask if they are permitted visitation with their grandson?"

Outraged, Edward shouted, "WHAT?! Of course, we demand to have time with him."

Shane gave Abby's hand a squeeze, happy that the judge was witness to the outburst.

The judge glared at him. "Mr. Martin, you will *not* shout in my chambers. If you refuse to comply, I can arrange for you to have overnight accommodations where you can spend time reflecting on how you should handle yourself in my presence. In the meantime, your visits with Devin will be in the presence of Ms. Stevens."

"Fine, our grandson will be ready. But I insist she be ordered to call us daily. I'm afraid she'll take him and go into hiding."

"Mr. Martin, I'm sure you are welcome to call her daily." Turning to address Abby, she said, "Ms. Stevens, are you agreeable?"

Pleased with how well the meeting had gone, Abby nodded.

"It sounds like we have a consensus," Judge Roy firmly stated.

Silence filled the room.

Kyle stood up. "Thank you, Your Honor."

"The caseworker will be in touch with all of you, and I will see everyone at the next hearing, where I expect to resolve this issue once and for all."

With a nod of dismissal, she turned her attention to a different stack of papers on her desk. With nothing left to say, the group filed out in silence.

Abby squeezed Shane's hand again as she floated on air out of the office. She looked around and found Devin sitting on a woman's lap. She hurried over and scooped him into her arms. Tears of relief fell unchecked down her cheeks onto the top of his little head. "Come on, little man. Let's go home."

15

$\mathcal{A}$bby parked the car in the Martin's driveway. They needed to stop there to pick up Devin's bags.

Abby pushed the doorbell, which Edward answered moments later. Tight-lipped, he pointed to the bags on the porch. "Take them and leave." Edward started to close the door in Abby's face, oblivious to the child in her arms, but then he added, "Young lady, we will be in touch on a daily basis, and you had better answer the phone when I call."

"Edward? Are you threatening me?" Abby snapped.

His face flushed with color at Abby using his first name. It threw him off-balance for a second, but he quickly recovered. "No. Just stating facts."

"Well, I have nothing to hide." Abby turned, her back straight and arms wrapped protectively around Devin. Shane stepped aside, gave Edward a curt nod, and followed her. He scooped up the bags as he walked past them.

Shane held the car door as she strapped the baby safely inside. Exhaustion rushed over her. "Would you please drive us home?"

"My pleasure, Abs."

She turned to gaze at the little boy who had fallen asleep the minute he got in his car seat. Her hand lightly rested on Shane's arm as they drove west on the highway, headed to Loudon. They had been driving for more than an hour when she started to relax. "I'm going to call your mom and let her know we're on the road. Maybe we could stop at What's Perkin' and pick up something for dinner. I don't have the energy to cook."

Shane pressed a speed-dial number and handed Abby the phone.

Cari answered on the third ring, "Hello?"

She pushed the speaker phone button. "Hi, Cari. We're on our way and should be home in a couple of hours with Devin," she said, happiness radiating in her voice.

"Thank heavens. That is the best news of the day. I won't ask for the details now, but when you feel up to it, I'd love to hear what happened. We are all so happy for you both."

"We're not out of the woods yet. We'll have to go back to court, and Social Services will be checking on me, but I'm confident everything will work out. My lawyer, Kyle Baird, said that unless there is a concern for Devin's welfare, the court should honor his parents' wishes."

Cari breathed a sigh of relief. "Kelly and Tim knew what they were doing when they chose you."

"I appreciate your support, Cari. It means more than you know. But I am calling to ask a favor. Do you have something at the shop that I could warm up for a light dinner? It has been a very long couple of days."

Without a moment's hesitation, Cari said, "You don't need to stop here, I'd be happy to drop it off. Do you need anything for the baby?"

"No, I'm all set. Thanks, Cari. I couldn't face having to deal with the grocery store after today."

"Don't give it another thought. Shane, drive safe and we'll talk tomorrow."

Abby thanked Cari again and told her where she could find the spare key. She disconnected and handed the phone to Shane.

"Why don't you rest your eyes? Devin is asleep, and you could use the rest too."

From behind dark glasses, Abby smiled. "That sounds like a good idea. I can recline and enjoy the warm sun. But just for a few minutes."

The next thing Abby knew, Shane was tapping her arm.

Speaking softly, he said, "Wake up, Sleeping Beauty."

"What? Where are we?" Abby bolted upright and adjusted her sunglasses. Glancing out the window, she discovered they were in her driveway.

"Well, I guess my eyes are rested. Jeez, I hope I didn't embarrass myself by snoring or drooling."

"Not that I noticed." He grinned. "Let's get the little man inside."

Abby unbuckled Devin and walked to the back door. Shane could hear the baby's gibberish as she opened the door. She was surprised to discover a large bouquet of flowers sitting on the table with a note from Cari and Ray. It read, "Welcome Home."

She smiled, appreciating the thoughtful gesture. She put Devin into his playpen and went back outside to help Shane unload the car. After a couple of trips, everything was in the house, and Devin was clamoring for attention.

"You're joining us for dinner, right?" Abby waited for Shane to nod before she added, "We should eat dinner out back. Devin can swing, and you can relax after the long drive." Abby gave Shane a firm hug. "Thank you for everything you've done, and Shane, I don't know how I would have gotten through the last thirty-six hours without you."

"You need to stop thanking me, Abby. I didn't do anything special. I was the chauffeur. Now, go." He waved her out the door. "I'll bring dinner out."

Alone in the kitchen, relief washed over him. Shane wasn't sure why this had been an emotional roller coaster for him. Abby was a good friend, and he was glad to be around to help her. It would have been hard for her to go through the ordeal alone, but what was he still doing at her house and getting dinner ready for them? Taking a couple of deep breaths, he watched Abby push Devin on the swing. A high-pitched baby laugh reached out to him in the kitchen. His heart contracted watching them and Shane shook off the odd feeling that had settled over him. After dinner, he would go home and get back into his routine. He picked up the dinner tray, pushed the door open with his backside, and called out, "Dinner!"

Abby's smile touched Shane's soft spot as he put the tray on the picnic table.

"Your mother's idea of a little something, I see?" She surveyed the various containers. "Everything looks scrumptious."

He shrugged. "Mom never does anything halfway. This is her idea of dinner, and it includes dessert. I can see Kate helped." Shane held up candles. "She thinks every meal should be by candlelight."

She started laughing so hard tears streamed down her cheeks. The sound captured Devin's attention, and he started to giggle, which prompted Abby to laugh even harder. It was contagious, and Shane joined the duo. The stress of the last few days evaporated as most of the meal disappeared.

Abby could see Devin rubbing his eyes. "It looks like someone is ready for bed. I'll get him settled in his crib, and we can watch a movie or play cards if you'd like to stay for a while?"

"Rain check? You could use a good night's sleep, too. I'm sure Devin will be up early." Shane carried the dirty dishes into the house, quickly getting the dishwasher loaded. "I'm going to head out."

Abby walked him to the door. He hesitated and leaned in to kiss her. Hovering a mere inch away, he said quietly, "You disturb me, Abby."

"Is that a compliment or a complaint?" she teased.

"Definitely a compliment." He leaned in closer and thoroughly kissed her goodnight.

16

*S*hane's night was a restless one. He had decisions to make regarding the direction his life seemed to be taking. He had spent the last several years wondering if the right girl would come around, but he had never expected to develop an attachment to a woman with a child. This circumstance didn't allow him to drift along, just having a good time. There were serious ramifications if his relationship with Abby continued. Was he ready for an instant family or was it best for all of them to keep the relationship platonic? He needed to keep a safe distance until it was all sorted out in his head.

He spent the day working hard, taxing his body. The hours flew by, and he didn't have to think about anything other than the next job. When it was time to head for home, his thoughts drifted to Abby, and he wondered what she was doing. He didn't have to wonder for long because he parked his truck next to her SUV in his driveway. The back hatch was open, but not a soul was in sight. What is she doing here? Shane wondered to himself.

He flung the truck's door open and strode around the

side of the house. A lone beach chair and an empty stroller sat side by side. Shane could see Devin was snuggled in Abby's lap. He quietly approached them, drinking in the view of woman and child. He stopped mid-step. Abby and Devin waiting for him— this was the view he longed to see every day, and the realization hit him like a ton of bricks. Unsure how to express what he was feeling, he brushed it aside. For the time being, he was going to concentrate on the moment.

Not wanting to scare her, Shane called out, "Hey, Abs."

She turned halfway in her chair, a smile graced her face. She was happy to see him.

"I hope you don't mind. I planned to leave before you got home, but it's so peaceful here, I guess I lost track of time. We've been watching the fish jump and just hanging out." Her megawatt smile that sparkled her blue-gray eyes.

Shane bent over to kiss her soft, upturned lips and then dropped a kiss on the baby's head.

"The lake is just sitting here, so come anytime," he stated. "Have you been here long?"

"About an hour or so. Devin woke up from a late nap. I guess from all the excitement, he was exhausted, and I thought, what the heck, might as well hang out at the beach. My new boss hasn't given me a key to the office, so I seized the opportunity to be lazy for the day," Abby joked.

"As a matter of fact, I bumped into your boss today, and he said you can take the rest of the week off and start on Monday." Shane kept his expression neutral. Despite his words, he was anxious for her to begin. He liked the idea of Abby spending her days at his house.

"I'd planned to start tomorrow and work a half day for

the rest of the week and then get into a regular schedule next week. To be honest, I don't want to have a lot of time on my hands to sit around worrying about the custody issue."

"If that's what you want, it's okay with me." He glanced toward the house. "Do you want to check out the office? But I have to warn you; I haven't had time to tidy it up."

"I'd love to see it." Abby held tight to the squirming child. Devin was lunging himself toward Shane.

He reached out and tucked his arm around him as they walked toward the house. Casually, Shane slipped his free hand into Abby's. "If you need something for the office, make a list, and I'll pick up whatever or you can stop at the store. Just save the receipts; I'll reimburse you."

Abby nodded in agreement. I'm curious what is behind the office door."

"You'll see." He gave her a sidelong look. "Do you have dinner plans?"

"As a matter of fact, I do."

A shock of surprise caught him off guard, causing Abby to try and hide a smirk.

"Kate and Ellie called, and we're getting together for dinner at my place around seven. After I get Devin tucked in for the night, we're having girl time."

*I*f Abby were honest, she'd admit that she didn't want to be alone, and she couldn't expect to have dinner with Shane again. She had monopolized his time for the last several days and nights. The lines were already blurred between their working relationship and personal life. She needed some time to make sure what she felt was real and not a reaction to the stress of the last few months. Spending time with Kate and Ellie and getting their perspective was the perfect plan. Abby didn't doubt Kate and Ellie would be straight with her, regardless of the fact that Shane was the topic of conversation, and their brother.

"That sounds like fun," Shane said.

She lightly punched his arm. "You'll see me tomorrow for work. Which brings me to a couple of questions. How do I get in the house and what time do you want me to start?"

"You can pick your own hours, but I do need you in the office on a somewhat regular schedule to answer customer calls and talk with suppliers. I'm usually gone by seven."

Shane dug in his pocket and pulled out a key. "This will open the kitchen door."

Abby took the key and dropped it into her pocket. "I can tell you're going to be the easiest boss I've worked for, McKenna. I'll work extra hard, so you don't regret hiring me." Abby walked into the office ahead of Shane.

"Abby, you moving back to Loudon is going to be good for all of us." Before she could respond, Shane skillfully switched the conversation to go over the ins and outs of his business.

❦

*A*bby heard a car in her driveway and pulled back the curtains. Kate and Ellie had just pulled in and parked. Devin was in his playpen, happily piling blocks around him under the watchful eye of his giant teddy bear. She had hoped to get him down for the night before the girls arrived, but the late nap changed her plan.

She went to greet her guests, keeping one ear open for unhappy tears. Flinging the door open, she greeted her friends, "Hello, girls. Something smells delicious."

Kate was carrying a large pot, and Ellie had a tray with an assortment of covered bowls.

"I do believe all the McKenna women are fantastic cooks," Abby exclaimed.

Ellie explained, "When you grow up with our mother, learning to cook is inevitable. She makes it look like so much fun, you want to cook with her."

Kate piped up, "When I was small, I would stand on a chair and help her." She set the pot on the stove, turning the flame on low.

Kate glanced around. "Where is that adorable little man? Is he in bed already?"

Abby pointed toward the living room. "He's in his playpen, in pajamas but not tired yet. He had a late nap. You can go see what he's doing, and I'll get some drinks."

"Can I give you a hand?" Ellie followed her into the kitchen.

Abby asked her to grab the appetizers from the refrigerator as she answered the ringing phone. Ellie made a quick exit to give her privacy.

Abby glanced at the caller ID and took a deep breath. "Hello?"

"Abigail, this is Edward Martin. I trust my grandson is well?"

"Yes, Edward. Devin is just fine. We spent part of the day outdoors, and before you ask, yes, he had sunscreen on." She controlled her temper and reminded herself she had encouraged these calls.

"What are your plans for tomorrow?"

The word "demanding" flashed in her brain. "I am

going into my office for a few hours, and I will be taking Devin with me. I have a porta crib and play area set up for him."

"Fine, I will speak with you tomorrow. I expect you to provide me with your office phone number tomorrow night. Goodnight, Abigail." Edward abruptly disconnected the call.

Abby stood in the kitchen holding the phone in her hand. "Edward, being a jerk isn't going to change the facts." She placed it on the table and went to join her friends.

Kate was sitting in the rocking chair with Devin on her lap. Twirling Kate's long dark hair around his chubby fingers, he gazed up at her in total bliss, fighting to keep his eyes open.

"I would really like to know what spell your family has cast to have this boy fall in love with everyone whose last name is McKenna," she mused. "I don't recall him ever taking to anybody like this, not even his grandparents." Abby shrugged. He was happy, and that was all that mattered.

Kate looked over his head. "He is a great judge of character."

The three girls quietly laughed, and Devin drifted off to dreamland.

"He is such a love," Ellie said as she watched her sister. "You're a natural with a baby in your arms."

Kate gave her a soft smile.

"Devin was good-natured from the minute he was born. Tears are reserved for hunger." Abby's smile dimmed. "Kelly did good, didn't she?"

"Yes, she did. I hope when Don and I are blessed with a baby we get as lucky," Kate said wistfully.

Abby discovered what Kate had been hiding: longing for a child of her own.

"Katie, how long have you and Don been trying?"

Ellie's head whipped around. How could Abby bring up a subject so obviously painful? No one dared ask her about having a baby.

Kate choked up and swallowed hard. "We've been trying for over a year to get pregnant. The doctor hasn't found anything wrong with either one of us. He says we're young and I need to relax and not to dwell on it. But each month comes and goes, and the color doesn't change on the stick."

Abby nodded, waiting for Kate to continue while she lent a sympathetic ear.

"We've talked about at what point we should give up and adopt. I guess we have plenty of time so, for now, we're going to let nature take its course. Occasionally, Don and I talk about it, but I try not to dwell. It makes us kind of sad, and I feel like I've let our families down, not giving them grandchildren." Kate wiped a lone tear from her cheek. "Thank goodness, Jake and Sara just had three. They'll keep Mom and Ray busy for a while." She gave a small, sad laugh. "Abby, I'm glad you asked. I wanted to tell you but didn't know how to bring up the subject, and I didn't want to burden you with all you have going on."

Abby squeezed Kate's knee. "Whenever you need to talk, I have time. Remember, we're BFFs for life."

"Kate?" Ellie lightly touched her sister on the arm. "I am so sorry. I always thought the topic of having babies should be avoided at all cost. Even though you never said anything, it was more what you didn't say that had me keep quiet. I should be a better sister to you and not shy away from painful subjects. But you need to remember, I'm an adult now and you can talk to me too."

Kate stammered, "Pixie, it's okay. I didn't want to talk about it; at least I hadn't until Abby asked. But you're right. I should have brought the subject up to you. It has gotten harder since the triplets were born. Holding them and Devin makes me think I've failed Don. He hasn't said he's disappointed, but I know he longs to have a baby too." Kate straightened her shoulders. "Don't worry; we're doing great and we'll get through this. I guess the timing is off or something. I have faith that someday we'll be blessed with children, but for now, honestly, I'm really fine."

"Kate, when you want to talk, I promise I'm ready to listen."

Kate looked at the little guy asleep in her arms. "I'm sure he would be more comfortable in his bed." She turned to Abby. "Do you mind if I take him up?"

"Of course, you can. Turn the night light on in his room and leave the door open a few inches," Abby replied.

Kate slid off the rocker and silently left the room with the precious boy.

"Let's get her mind off babies. Are you hungry?" Abby glanced toward the stairs.

Ellie was quick to agree. "Absolutely."

Kate returned and discovered the coffee table was laden with food. "Oh, this will be fun, eating on the floor, very informal. Good idea, ladies."

The girls relaxed on the floor, wine glasses close by. "Ellie, have you thought about what you're going to do after graduation?" Abby asked. "I remember when I was graduating I was at a complete loss on what my future held."

"Abby? This is Kyle Baird." Involuntarily, she held her breath.

"Hi, Kyle. I wasn't expecting to hear from you so soon."

"I wanted to let you know Social Services will be contacting you very shortly. You can expect that they will send someone to inspect your home and office since Devin doesn't go to daycare. It is their job to verify he is well cared for and in a safe environment."

She dropped into a chair. "I didn't realize they would want to see where I work."

"Since your office is in a private home, the Martin's have specifically asked to have it inspected. It is in your best interest to oblige any request. Complete transparency is very important. We don't want to appear like there is something to hide."

"I don't have anything to hide, Kyle. You know that. Can't you assure them my boss has made it very comfortable and safe for Devin?"

"Abby, we don't want to put up any roadblocks. Remember what is at stake: custody of Devin. We have to continue to be open and honest. Now, I don't know when exactly you'll get the visits, but I wanted you to be prepared." In an attempt to reassure her, he added, "Abby, trust me. Everything is going to be fine. I know we've been through hell and back with losing Tim and Kelly. I didn't just lose a client; I lost a good friend and I'll continue to protect his son."

She moved papers around on the desk and then crossed to the window.

"I don't know how much more stress I can bear."

"This will be over soon. Once the final reports are submitted to the court, Judge Roy will review them and then make her ruling. When this is over, you can move on with your life." He waited for Abby to say something. Hearing nothing but silence, he asked, "Have you heard from the Martin's since you've been home?"

With a huff she said, "Oh yes. Edward calls daily and never at the same time. Typically, the conversation lasts a minute or two. He calls my house, cell, and now the office number, hurls a few nasty comments, and then reminds me he'll be calling the next day and that I'd better answer. I guess they're making sure I haven't run off with the baby."

"Do you want me to speak to the judge and let her know they're harassing you?"

"No." She gasped. Her stomach clench with fear. "That will only make things worse. Isn't it ironic? I guess that's what I should have done to them after I dropped Devin off, called them constantly."

"Abby, stop. You didn't have any reason to suspect how far they would go to get what they wanted. Tim's parents are used to being in control. He stripped that away from them with his final wishes."

"I guess you're right. But I should have had a clue, especially when they told me about the nanny." She remembered Kelly saying her in-laws thought they were above everyone else. "Heaven only knows how Tim turned out to be such a good man." Abby sighed. "Anyway, thank you for calling, Kyle. I'll be waiting for my inspection." She laughed ruefully.

After telling Abby he would stay in touch, Kyle disconnected.

She sat down and leaned back in her office chair and gazed out the window. Movement caught her attention.

She hesitated before getting up to get a better look; a large doe and her fawn cautiously crept through the grass, intent on getting to the water's edge. She didn't move for fear of them hearing her. She watched for several minutes. The doe kept the baby between her and the house, shielding him from potential harm. Suddenly, the doe popped her head up, alert, and waited briefly before she and the baby bounded gracefully out of sight, into the woods. The office phone rang, reminding her it was a working day.

"Hello, McKenna Landscaping. This is Abby, may I help you?"

A deep warm laugh greeted her. "I like how you answer the phone. You make it sound very official like it's a big business or something. Hiring you might have been the best decision I've made for my company in a long time."

"Hello, stranger. It's been a while. You must be very busy?"

"*You* have no idea." Shane couldn't tell Abby he was busy avoiding her. Until he knew what his next step was, it was better this way. However, the longing to hear her voice was uncontrollable.

When he got home each night, Shane drank in the smell from her perfume. It lingered in the air. He sat in the office, careful not to disturb her piles. He was impressed at how fast she was creating order from his chaos. He could picture her now, sitting in the same chair. Focus, he chided himself. What was Abby saying?

"Have you seen the office? It's coming along nicely.

"Nope just bring yourself. See you in a while."

He could hear a baby cry as Jake hung up the phone.

Shane drove from where he was parked to the liquor store to grab a six-pack. He stopped at Blake's Farmers Market and bought Sara flowers. He parked on the street and circled around to the back of the house, where he found Jake closing the top of the smoking grill.

"Excellent. Cold beverages." Jake reached out and took an icy bottle from Shane.

He busied himself at the grill while Shane sat in a deck chair legs outstretched, stewing.

After his bottle was empty, Jake looked over but doubted Shane was going to talk. "So, you got something on your mind?"

Shane took a deep pull of his beer. "How did you know Sara was, well, you know, the girl for you?"

"Well," Jake said thoughtfully, "I thought about her constantly, I wanted to spend all my free time with her, and it didn't matter what we were doing or where we were going. Pretty girls could walk by, and I was oblivious. She was everything I didn't know I wanted." He had a faraway look in his eyes, seeming to remember the early days when they started dating.

"One day I was working in Dad's shop, and she was at school. I asked myself what I was doing—she was there, and I was here. I dropped what I was doing, hopped in my car, and drove straight to her dorm. I sat in the lobby and waited for hours, not sure what time she'd be back but knowing that eventually, she would walk through the lobby. Finally, she came in, and she was surprised to see me. I picked her up, twirled her around, and kissed her like it was the first time. She laughed so hard tears streamed down her face. And then she asked me what took me so long to make up my mind." Jake paused and looked at his brother. "I pretended like I didn't know what she was talking about. But she had known right from the beginning that we belonged together. Man, she is the beat of my heart. She's my home." Jake stopped talking, having nothing left to say.

Shane sat there, an empty bottle in his hand.

Stating the obvious Jake said, "You got it bad, bro."

"I guess I do. I didn't think I would ever find someone that would dominate each waking moment. It seems like I was headed in her direction this whole time. Everyone I met up until now was getting me ready for Abby. What do I do now? She is responsible for her sister's kid. Am I ready to take that responsibility on too?"

With a hearty laugh, Jake said, "Don't waste a minute here; get over there, twirl her around, and tell her you plan on doing it for the rest of your lives."

"I can't barge in. She's probably getting Devin ready for bed. We have a date on Friday. That will give me time to figure out what I can say to convince her to give me a chance."

Inside the house, three little babies started exercising their lungs.

"Duty calls. Come on; there's a little kid that needs to have some uncle time."

Jake turned off the grill. "Eventually, we'll feed you dinner. This is our life, not as much twirling around as there used to be, but I wouldn't trade this for anything. I'm a lucky man."

Shane clapped Jake on his shoulder and chuckled. "Lead the way, bro."

18

The family was thrilled; Abby had a date with Shane on Friday night and he had asked if Kate and Don would babysit. Kate was so excited that she didn't waste any time saying yes. The moment she had gotten off the phone she sent a group text to her mom, Ellie, and Sara. Everyone suspected big news was brewing for Shane and Abby. The family had a friendly wager going on as to how long it would take for Shane to do something major.

Ellie said she thought he would wait until the custody fiasco was behind Abby. Kate figured he'd say something on their date and Cari thought it would take a long time for him to make Abby and Devin an official part of the family. Traditionally, her son was a slow mover.

No one agreed on the timing, but they all knew Shane had found the love of his life. Over the years, Cari had watched her son date, never bringing a girl home for family events or becoming involved in a long-term relationship. He treated the girls he dated with respect, and he was honest with each one, telling them he wasn't looking for a commitment. Cari had worried about his inability to connect with someone and have a long-term romance. She felt responsible; her late husband, Ben, had died when the kids were young. Before Shane had the chance to witness the deep love they had shared. Cari didn't want her son to fritter away his life. She knew better than anyone that you don't get do-overs. You get one chance. It was a long time before Cari had found love again. She and Ray had tap-danced around their feelings for years, and they had almost lost their chance. It was time they couldn't ever get back.

With the lunch rush over, Abby wheeled Devin into the shop. Cari pointed to what had become Abby's table.

Devin was strapped into the high chair where he was happily waving his chubby hands at Cari. It had been a few weeks since she had stopped in for coffee and to catch up with the girls.

Cari walked over with the coffee pot and three mugs, setting them down to pour.

"You don't need to wait on me, Cari."

"You've got your hands full, and I remember what it was like having kids. All I wanted was for someone to pour me coffee in a clean cup I didn't have to wash." Cari smiled at the young woman. "Would you mind some company? Kate and I could use a break."

She plopped the tote bag on the floor. "Of course, we'd love the company. If you didn't visit, Devin would put up a fuss to get your attention," she laughed.

Cari tweaked Devin's cheek. "And I would have come right over to see the little angel."

Kate wiped her hands on a towel as she walked over. Her long dark hair was swept up in a knot on the top her head, and her green eyes were sparkling. Delight splashed across her face.

"Hi, you two. What brings you in today? You're not working?"

Kate gracefully sat on the chair and sipped the coffee in front of her.

"We're taking a break away from the office, even though it has a beautiful view. Devin said he needed a cookie from his favorite shop. So, we packed up, put the answering machine on, left Shane a message and here we are."

"Isn't that a coincidence? I made sugar cookies, which have just a touch of frosting on them, just enough to make him a sticky mess." Kate hopped up to retrieve cookies, sliced cake, and a tart from the case.

She set the plate down, and Devin strained to get his hands on the treats that were just out of his reach. Giving Kate a sloppy grin, he wiggled his fingers and babbled. Kate broke a cookie into quarters and handed him two pieces.

Abby cleared her throat, suddenly nervous. "I have to admit; I do have another reason for stopping in." She looked from Cari to Kate. "Shane has asked me out for dinner and a movie, so I need a sit—"

Before she could finish, Kate interrupted. "Sure! I'm happy to babysit. Just give me the details."

Cari interjected, "Ray and I would love to watch him again. He can sleep at our house too if you'd like to have the entire evening to yourself."

Abby couldn't help but laugh. She turned to the baby. "Devin, the ladies are fighting over you already." Then to Cari and Kate, she said, "You all might have other plans; it's this Friday."

Kate spoke up. "We're free, and if you'd like, bring the porta-crib, and he can spend the night. We don't have any plans for Saturday."

"Oh, that sounds tempting. If we catch a movie, it might be late. I wouldn't want to keep you guys up too late. Are you sure? You want to keep him overnight? He can sleep just about anywhere as long as he has his blankie."

She had to wonder if Kate and Cari were dying to get details.

"Now that your sitter is lined up, tell us, what's the big date with Shane? I thought you said he hadn't been around much since your trip to Boston."

"He called the office yesterday to check in, hung up, and then called back two minutes later. He asked me if I wanted to have dinner and go to the movies. When he suggested one of you might watch Devin, I agreed. Under the condition that it was okay with one of you."

Hoping to sound nonchalant, Abby focused her attention on Devin.

"Sounds like fun. What movie are you going to see?" Cari tried to keep the conversation light.

"I have no idea, but as long as he doesn't want to see a horror movie, I'm good."

"Do you remember the Cornwall drive-in? It's open for the season. You could have a light dinner and then see a double feature. I think they have a couple of screens. Let's check to see what's playing." Kate grabbed her laptop from the counter and sat back down. "Don't let Shane pick the movie; you'll see some war thing. Comedy would be much better for a date."

Cari jumped in. "Since Kate's taking the baby

overnight, you won't need to rush. And when was the last time you went to the drive-in?"

"Let me send Shane a text; maybe he doesn't want to go to a drive-in. It does sound like fun, and I've never been, sounds like something teenagers do." Abby was getting excited; Friday was shaping up to be a lot of fun.

"I'll text Shane and see if he's okay with a comedy in Cornwall."

Kate studied the screen and said, "Perfect. There is the new animated film with dinosaurs and the second feature is a comedy about circus performers. Entertaining yet low key and it's just the ticket. No pun intended."

Abby's phone blinked, and she scanned the text. "He said, 'sounds like fun,' and that the movie's my choice. That was easy. Any idea if there's a place close by to eat first?"

Cari spoke up. "I'm not sure. Ray has been working out that way; I'll give him a call." She moved to the kitchen.

After a few minutes Cari returned to the table. "Ray said there is a family-style Italian restaurant five minutes from the drive-in. Good food, reasonably priced, and very popular. He's had lunch there and said it was excellent."

Abby jotted down the information and slipped the paper into her handbag.

"Date night is planned; it's casual and perfect. I'll fill Shane in later." She tapped out a short message and put the phone away.

"The other night, Ellie was saying she's finishing college at the end of the summer. Are you going to have a party for her? Finishing a year early is quite an accomplishment."

"Parties and the McKenna-Davis family go hand in hand. We have to celebrate because it's going to be a long time until there is another graduation in the family. Ellie's worked hard, a double major in three years." Cari beamed. "I'm very proud of her."

"I'd love to help if you don't mind. I'm getting to know the grown-up version of Ellie, and she's terrific. When we were kids, she followed Kate and me everywhere. I'm sorry to say there were times we weren't very nice to her." Abby realized that, despite the tragedy that brought her back to Loudon, life had taken her in a new direction and brought her home to wonderful old friends.

Teasing, Kate said, "Why would you think you wouldn't get recruited as kitchen help? Guess you forgot how we roll around here, chicklet. All for one and one for all!" she teased.

Kate smirked while Cari gave her the "mom" look.

"Are you trying to send Abby running for Boston again, missy?"

"Not to worry, Mom. Abby can dish it out and take it," Kate said playfully.

"Ah, remember," Abby said in her best menacing tone, "payback, my friend, payback." Unable to contain herself, she burst out laughing. The sound was so unexpected Devin looked up with his cookie-smeared face and started clapping his hands and putting in his two cents of gibberish.

Within seconds, the three women and a small boy were all laughing. The door jingled, catching them off-guard. Cari looked up, dabbing her eyes with a napkin. She was happy to see Shane and Don step through the doorway. Abby and Kate struggled to compose themselves.

The guys took one look and shook their heads. "Do you have any idea what we interrupted?" Don asked, nodding his head in the direction of his wife and mother-in-law.

"I have no idea, but something tells me they're up to no good." Shane's gaze over his sister, to his mother, and then rested on Abby who dabbing tears away from the corners of her eyes.

"Who's going to fill us in on the joke?" Shane looked around the group. Silence answered him. "Don, I guess the joke is on us." With a devilish look, he grinned at Abby. "For now."

She shivered under his gaze, her insides getting tied in knots. Changing the subject was the prudent thing to do.

"We're all set for Friday night. Kate is watching Devin at her house." She glanced at Don. "Well, that's if Don's okay with the plan."

"We're happy to look after the little guy. I guess you have a crib or something for him?"

"Yes, I do. Of course, if there's an issue, I'll come get him. I told Kate he sleeps just about anywhere, so I don't think it will be a problem."

"We'll be fine. Don's an uncle on his side of the family. His sister Liza has two boys and it will be great practice for us when the triplets get a little older, and they come to stay with Auntie Kate and Uncle Don." Kate smiled broadly.

Abby knew it was hiding an ache in her heart.

"Alright then, it's settled. I'll bring him over around four. I'll get the porta-crib up and then slip home to get ready." Her eyes met Shane's.

"What time should I pick you up?" He was happy to have Abby handle the details.

She lit up. "Around six. There is an Italian restaurant that your parents recommended for dinner. It's about five miles from the movies. The weather is supposed to be perfect, so I thought a drive-in would be fun. The first feature is a cartoon, the second is a comedy, and the third movie, if we're still awake, is an old Three Stooges flick."

He grinned. "Mosquitos?" he teased.

"I'll bring a can of bug spray, just to be on the safe side."

"Sounds good. Is the restaurant casual?"

"Yes, it's a family place. But if Italian doesn't sound appealing, we can go somewhere else."

"No, I love Italian." He didn't want to change a thing.

"Don, let's grab those cookies and iced tea. We're planting trees this afternoon, and its thirsty work. Abby, when you get back to the office, will you call the garden center and confirm delivery for the Jones's place? They should deliver first thing in the morning. I'm expecting the shrubs and a couple of Chinese maples. Tomorrow, we need to finish the perennial gardens as well. If they can't deliver, give me a call, and I'll swing by later today."

"You got it, boss." In jest, Abby gave him a jaunty salute. She was impressed with how his mind clicked off details for specific jobs.

"Before I go back, I need to pick up a few office supplies. I want to get an external hard drive to back up the computer files and a few other things." She pulled a list out of her handbag and passed it to Shane. "Do you need anything while I'm there?"

She wanted the office ready for an influx of new business. She thought McKenna Landscaping could branch into vintage garden design. Before she said anything, she was going to research suppliers and the sales potential.

"Nope, I don't need anything. I have an account at Village Office; I'll give them a call and list you as an authorized buyer on my account." Shane excused himself and placed a short call. He gave her a thumbs-up. "You're all set; get what you need."

Abby glanced at her watch. "I should be at the office in about an hour."

"Good. I'll check in later. Don, are you ready?"

"Yup, I've got cookies and iced tea, and if you're lucky, I'll share."

Kate walked with Don and Shane to the curb, kissing her husband on the cheek and reminding him to be careful. She watched as they pulled away from the curb. A woman caught Kate's attention. She was well dressed in a dark business suit and heels. She held up her hand in an attempt to capture Kate's attention.

19

"*E*xcuse me. I was hoping you could give me directions."

Kate waited for the woman on the sidewalk.

"I'm looking for 1783 Main Street and Abigail Stevens."

"May I ask what your business is with Ms. Stevens?" Kate politely inquired.

"I'm sorry; it's of a personal nature."

"I'm sorry. Ms. Stevens is a dear friend, and I'm not comfortable giving out personal information to strangers. I'm sure you can understand." Kate stood between the woman and the door to What's Perkin'.

"I appreciate you protecting her privacy, but I do need to speak with her. It's very important." She pulled a business card from her pocket. "Would you give her my card and ask her to call me on my cell?"

Kate paused to read it.

NOREEN LANDRY, MASSACHUSETTS DEPARTMENT OF SOCIAL SERVICES

"Oh, are you here to do a home inspection?" Kate asked.

A surprised look flashed over her face. Ms. Landry sniffed at Kate's tone of voice, then said, "I guess that's how some people refer to it. I take my job very seriously. Making sure a child has a safe and secure home with a loving guardian is my top priority."

Kate glanced at the card. "I'm sorry if I offended you, Ms. Landry. Around here, we look after our friends and neighbors."

"I'm sure that can be a good thing, but right now I need to talk to Ms. Stevens. Would you please have her call me?"

Before Kate could answer, Abby emerged from the shop, pushing the stroller in front of her.

"Excuse me, Kate." Abby gave the woman a warm smile, thinking she was overdressed for this heat. "I'm sorry to interrupt but I'm going to the store, and then I'm heading back to the office. I'll see you tomorrow?"

Kate put her hand on her arm. "Abby, this is Ms. Landry. She's from the Department of Social Services."

Instantly, Abby recognized the name and extended her hand. "Hello, I'm Abigail Stevens. My lawyer, Mr. Baird, told me to expect you."

*N*oreen Landry firmly shook the outstretched hand. The young woman standing before her wasn't what she had expected. Abigail Stevens looked young but wore an air of maturity. The baby was chattering nonsense a mile a minute, playing with the toys attached to the tray of his stroller. Noreen Landry had learned that a first impression at a surprise visit was typically a good indication of what might be going on behind the scenes. The baby looked happy and in good health.

"Ms. Stevens, I hope you understand part of my job is to show up unannounced to see the actual environment the child is exposed to on a daily basis. I'm sure you can understand."

"Absolutely. I have nothing to hide." Abby pointed to the south end of the street. "If you'd like, we can walk to our home. It's not far, and I could show off parts of the town on the way."

"That is an excellent suggestion, Ms. Stevens."

"Please, call me Abby." She took a deep breath and exhaled.

Noreen was sure there was a bucket of nerves raging inside the young woman. "Thank you..." she hesitated, "Abby."

"If you could give me just a moment, I'd like to call my boss and let him know I'll be delayed."

Abby pushed the stroller to Kate. "Would you mind watching him for a minute? I'm going to leave a message for Shane."

She stepped away from Ms. Landry to use her cell phone. Kate pulled the stroller close. Noreen was quick to notice the gesture and made a mental note.

"Ready?" Abby asked as she rejoined the ladies.

Noreen nodded. As they walked down Main Street, she seized the opportunity to ask some routine questions about the baby's care, being a single parent, and even inquired whether Abby was angry that her sister had left Devin in her care. Noreen made it sound more like small talk, interjecting comments about the town and Abby's support system.

· · ·

*S*o, it begins, Abby thought. She had mentally prepared for an interrogation, but this was a bit more relaxed. "I believe I've adjusted to the changes as well as anyone could expect. Within the last three years, I've lost both my parents and sister. I didn't have a support system in Boston, and it was lonely living in my sister's house. I didn't have close friends, and I decided to leave my job until I knew what I wanted to do next. Fortunately, my parents had kept our home. It was our escape from the hustle and bustle a couple of weekends a few times in the year. It was an easy decision to sell everything and move. I've reconnected with my best friend and her family, got a decent paying job where I can take Devin with me, and above all, we have a fresh start." Abby paused.

"But were you upset with your sister? Her desire for you to raise her son has changed the course of your life."

She could feel the smile leave her face. "Of course, I'm angry, but not with Kelly. A senseless car accident took Kelly and Tim, the last of my family. They knew how much I love Devin and they were the only family I had left. Despite the circumstances, I'm honored they would entrust me with their beloved son. I have never for a minute been angry they chose me."

Abby turned into the yard, and Noreen followed. She was taking notice of the neat walkway that led to the side door. Abby turned the key in the lock while Noreen peeked into the backyard.

"Would you like to look around the backyard?" Abby suggested. "I had a swing installed for Devin. There is plenty of room for a sandbox and full swing set for when he gets a little bigger."

Through Noreen's eyes, Abby could see it was well

maintained and had plenty of room for play equipment. "I've always liked a shady backyard. The outside of your home is beautiful."

"Let's go inside." Abby moved through the doorway into the dimly lit kitchen. She set the baby in his high chair and removed glasses from the cabinet.

"Iced tea or lemonade?" Abby inquired.

"Tea, please." Noreen sat down in the spacious, tidy kitchen. A large window dominated the back wall that overlooked the yard.

"So, I understand Edward and Louise Martin believe you should be relieved of your guardianship of Devin Martin."

"I guess they are upset that Tim and Kelly made the decision to have me raise Devin. Honestly, I don't understand why they are adamant they would be better guardians. Many times, I've asked them to spend time with us, to come out and stay the weekend. I want them in Devin's life. He is their only child's son."

Noreen made a note in her folder. She looked up and said, "If you don't mind, I would like to see the rest of the house."

"Not at all, it's a bit rambling for just the two of us." Abby picked up the baby. "Let's start in Devin's room."

Noreen scrutinized each room, taking in every minute detail. Each room was clean, neat, and tidy, and, most important, safe for a child. The electrical plugs were covered with safety devices, and all breakable items were out of reach. They got to Devin's room. "I didn't expect his room would be so beautifully decorated."

"I know the rest of the house looks slightly outdated, but the nursery was freshly painted and had furniture that would grow with him. I wanted it to be special for him."

Devin spied his favorite teddy bear in the corner of his crib. Babbling, he stretched out his hands. Abby plucked the bear out of the crib and tucked it safely into his chubby arms. He screeched with glee and proceeded to chew on the bear's nose, chattering a mile a minute in his own language. Abby chuckled as if understanding every word that he said.

"Well, I think I've seen enough here. Do you think we could go to your office? I'd like to see the environment Devin is in during the day."

Happy to oblige, Abby said, "We can stop at the shop, pick up our cars, and then drive to the office. I work out of the business owner's home."

"I read that in the report. Frankly, if your home is any indication of the office, I don't foresee anything that would give me cause for concern. However, there will be a few more in-home visits. I need to follow procedure."

"Of course." Abby was pleased that this seemed to be going well.

❦

It crossed Noreen's mind that if all the children she was assigned to were half as lucky as this little boy, it would put her out of business. She surmised this was a case of disgruntled grandparents with too much time and money on their hands.

Noreen pulled into Shane's driveway and got out of her car where Abby held Devin in her arms. Surprised at the location of the office, she said, "This is lovely." Noreen slowly looked over the manicured lawn and drank in the view of the lake.

"If it's nice, we have lunch outside, go for a walk, and then Devin is ready for a nap, and I can work."

She opened the door and stepped into the great room.

Noreen stepped inside quickly, noting the playpen and other baby items in the main living area.

"Does your employer live here full time?" she quizzed.

"Yes, he does. Shane is on job sites during the day, so Devin and I have the place to ourselves. My office is toward the back." Abby led the way down the hall. She propped open the office door, moving inside to allow Noreen to enter.

"May I look around?" She noticed the baby monitor on the desk and the outlet covers.

"Of course. I would ask that we respect Shane's privacy. His bedroom is at the end of the hallway."

"Does the baby have access to that room?"

"No. Devin could be in my office, the great room, or upstairs. Shane allowed me to put a crib in a spare room."

Surprised, Noreen asked, "Your boss allows you to put Devin's things in the main living area and install a crib in a spare bedroom? That's quite a boss."

She cocked her head. "I grew up with the McKenna's. You met Kate at the coffee shop, where she works with her mother. When I moved home, I wanted a job, and Shane needed someone he could trust to run his office. I wasn't ready to put Devin into daycare, and he understood, as he recently became an uncle to a set of triplets. It was his suggestion to bring Devin with me."

"Well, I believe I have enough information to start my report. I appreciate your flexibility today." Noreen reached out and shook Abby's hand. She turned to leave and stopped. "Abby, may I speak off the record? I think your sister and brother-in-law made the right choice. It is obvious to me that you love Devin, and the degree that you've changed your life to accommodate his needs is admirable. We will meet a couple more times, but I am already impressed. I wish all the cases I had were so straightforward." Noreen Landry walked out to her car without looking back.

Abby kissed the sleeping baby nestled on her shoulder. She whispered, "Devin, nobody realizes I'm the lucky one."

20

*A*bby pulled up to Kate and Don's at four on the dot. Their house—a picture-perfect cottage—sat on the outskirts of town. Kate burst through the door with Don close behind.

"Hi there!" Abby waved as she began pulling several bags and the porta crib from the back of her SUV.

Don scooped up the bags and crib and carried them into the house. Abby unstrapped Devin, passing him to Kate as she unhooked his seat from the safety belts.

"I'm going to leave the car seat, just in case."

"We don't plan on going anywhere, but it's a good idea. You can set it inside the front entryway." Kate passed Don as she walked toward the house while softly talking to the baby.

Don returned. "Does anything else need to come inside?" He took the car seat from Abby.

"No, that's all there is. I got carried away, not sure what to pack. I had to remind myself it's for only one night." Abby laughed nervously. "This is the first time I've left him with anyone other than his grandparents. And we all know how that turned out."

Kate reached out to her. "Try not to worry, Devin will be fine. We plan to do our best and spoil him rotten while he's here," Kate teased.

"I guess it's good that you're only going to have him overnight. It won't give you much time to create a little monster." She laughed with her friends.

Abby showed Don how to set up the crib, and she put the baby monitor on the dresser. She prayed the baby slept through the night for them. Satisfied with the set-up, Abby joined Kate in the living room where she was having quite a conversation with Devin. She leaned against the door-jamb and watched the two of them.

She cleared her throat, suppressing a giggle, she said, "Are you ready for me to head out so you can start spoiling him?"

"I already started," Kate quipped. "Seriously, Abs, I hope you guys have a great time tonight. You and my brother make a nice couple."

"I'm not sure if it's going anywhere, but for the moment, I'm enjoying myself. He's easy to be around. I'm sure it's because we've known each other since we were kids."

"I think it's a combination of things—your past, where you are today, and the promise of your future," Kate surmised.

"What do you mean? I don't think Shane is interested in a future with me; I have baggage. Don't get me wrong; I wouldn't change it for anything, but Devin and I are a package deal."

"Honey, we all have baggage in one form or another. From the minute we're born, we start accumulating it. But it's how we handle it. You handle your baggage with grace and strength, and you do it head-on. That's something I admire."

Abby sank down on the sofa. "Kate, do you think I might have a future with Shane?"

"Do you want a future, a life with him?" Kate pushed.

"When I'm with him, I can't even begin to describe it. He makes me feel whole, like I belong again. I've been lost since my parents and Kelly died. When I moved back to Loudon, I hoped to reconnect with you. I've discovered so much more. Your family figuratively wrapped their arms around Devin and me. I don't feel alone anymore. But with Shane, it's so much more than that. When he kissed me for the first time, it felt like I had come home." Abby's eyes searched Kate's. "Does that make any sense?"

She nodded. "It's how I feel when Don kisses me, and no matter what is going on, he's my center. With Don by my side, I can get through anything." She paused. "Including infertility."

"Kate, give yourself some more time. You're putting a lot of pressure on yourself." She reached out to take Kate's hand.

"That is a conversation for another day. Right now, we're talking about you and my brother."

"With that whole mess in Boston, if Shane hadn't been with me, I would have muddled through it somehow. Instead, because of him, I was strong and ready to fight tooth and nail for Devin."

"I think you're giving him a little too much credit. Devin means the world to you. You would do anything to protect him. Do you have any idea how Shane feels about you?"

"I'm not sure. He's comfortable with Devin, which is a

good thing. I guess he's interested in me." With that statement, Abby got up from the sofa and scooped up Devin. "I don't know where this relationship is going. I'm going to enjoy the time I spend with him and not think about anything else."

She kissed Devin. "Be a good boy for Auntie Kate." She passed him back. "I'll see you tomorrow around noon?"

"Take your time; we're here whenever you're ready to pick him up. Maybe we can go out to the lake. We can have a picnic."

Abby hugged Kate and Devin. "I'll think about it, but Shane may have had enough time with me after tonight. Don't hesitate to call if there are *any* problems."

She felt a pang of sadness as she drove toward her house. She had never left Devin with anyone. Shrugging away her mood, her thoughts turned to the evening with Shane. She planned to wear jeans, a pale gray silk blouse, and a matching sweater. Despite the daytime temperatures, the evenings turned cool, and she wanted to be comfortable during the movies. She glanced at her watch. It was time to put a wiggle on it. Shane would be coming to pick her up in less than an hour.

A quick rap on the door gave Abby a half-second to put on a final dab of lip gloss. She found Shane standing on the front porch and looking heart-stoppingly handsome. His deep blue eyes sparkled with excitement. He wore a light purple pullover shirt that set off his deeply tanned arms. A small tuft of chest hair set Abby's blood racing and heart pounding.

· · ·

*S*hane was speechless. He wondered how this woman spent all day working, taking care of a baby, and still looked amazing. Her hair hung in short loose waves, framing her heart-shaped face. He wanted to reach out, cup the back of her neck, run his hands through her hair, and drown her with a deep kiss. His gut constricted with desire. How was he going to spend the evening with her and keep his true feelings under wraps?

"Are you ready?" he said in a low, sexy voice, implying more than dinner and a movie.

"I, um, I'm going to get my sweater." Visibly flustered, Abby left him standing on the porch.

Once Abby pulled the door closed, they strolled to the curb. Shane stole a sideways glance or two, enjoying her profile, entranced by her long eyelashes.

The drive to the restaurant seemed to fly by. Shane didn't want to share Abby with anyone, even a room full of strangers. He enjoyed Abby's running commentary on points of interest during the drive. It would have calmed his nerves if he realized her one-sided conversation was an attempt to soothe her butterflies.

They walked hand in hand to the main entrance. They moved to one side as a couple came out, laughing and moving toward the parking lot. The man stopped and called out, "Shane?"

He turned. "Wow, James, look at you!" Shane extended his hand and gave the newcomer a hearty shake. "It's been, what, four years?" Shane quizzed.

"Abby, this is James Wells. He worked for me when I started my landscaping business. James, this is Abby Stevens."

"It's a pleasure to meet you, Abby. This is my wife,

Mary. We're celebrating. We just found out we're having a little boy."

Shane hugged Mary and clapped James on the back. "Congratulations to you both."

Abby grinned. "Congratulations. You must be so excited."

"We're going to see our parents and tell them to return anything they might have bought in pink! Enjoy your evening!" James shouted as he and Mary waved good-bye and hurried to their car.

"Shall we?" Shane held the door for Abby, ushering her in ahead of him.

The host greeted them. "Do you have a reservation?"

"Yes, McKenna."

The host checked the book on the podium. "Right this way, please."

He escorted them to a quiet corner away from several large gatherings. The host lit a candle on the red-and-white checked tablecloth and silently withdrew, allowing Shane to hold Abby's chair.

Abby casually glanced around the dining room. It was buzzing with activity.

Shane's eyes followed hers. "The food must be good. This place is rocking." Shane flipped open the menu and was pleasantly surprised to discover his favorite, linguine with clam sauce, was listed as a house specialty. Easiest decision of the night, he thought.

Abby studied the menu carefully, her forehead wrinkled with concentration. A waiter set a breadbasket down and poured water. Before the waiter could ask, Shane asked for a few more minutes. "We're not quite ready to order." The waiter nodded and moved to another table.

The aromas mingled in the room. "This is a tough decision. The items listed on the menu look amazing and the smells in this room are making my mouth water. Should I go overboard and order fettuccini and shrimp, or something lighter?" She glanced at Shane.

"I'm sorry I'm taking so long to decide. Everything sounds so good. Do you see something you like?" she asked.

Nodding, eyes locked on hers. "And I've decided what I'm going to have for dinner, too."

Stammering, Abby said, "What?"

Shane found her shyness charming. "Linguini, and you."

"Fettuccini," she added simply, doing her best to ignore the double entendre.

The waiter returned and took their order. Abby kept the conversation light, as she launched into the story about her visit with Noreen Landry. She shared the details of Kate being overprotective at the shop, as well as other moments from the rest of the meeting.

"When I think about it, I have to laugh. Kate wasn't going to let anyone get near us. I felt a little better when Ms. Landry said she could see why Kelly and Tim made the choice to ask me to care for Devin. With all the support from your family, I'm not as worried about the hearing. I'm anxious to get it behind us, and hopefully, I'll never have to worry about anyone trying to take Devin away from me."

"After it's over, you and Devin can move on with your life." Shane reached across the table, covering her hand with his, lightly caressing it. "So, how do you like your job?"

"Now that I have the office set up to operate efficiently, I have a couple of ideas I'd like to bounce off you."

"I'm listening."

"I think there may be untapped business potential in creating gardens with a vintage theme. You could use heirloom varieties of edible flowers, herbs, and vegetables. Historical homes are prevalent in our area, and I don't see any other companies offering that type of service."

"That's an interesting idea. What exactly do you mean by 'vintage'?"

"People used to share cuttings and save seeds, and gardens had multiple purposes. Some perennials were herbs and medicinal plants, which can be dried for use in tea and tinctures. We could incorporate kitchen gardens and make them part of an overall design, instead of the rectangular patch that doesn't have a good plan so each year it becomes a weedy mess. I'd be happy to design something for my backyard to give you an idea of what I have had running around in my brain. Besides, my yard desperately needs some work!"

He continued to hold her hand. Unwilling to let go. "You have some good ideas. I'm not sure what you mean by a kitchen garden, though."

"Ah, well, they are defined garden areas that typically have a geometric pattern. The plants are chosen not just for functionality but also to be aesthetically pleasing. Often, edible flowers and herbs are planted with vegetables. It can be quite beautiful."

Shane smiled at Abby's enthusiasm. "Definitely something we should explore in greater detail. Let's talk about it when we're back in the office, run some numbers, and see if there's a decent profit margin in vintage gardens."

The waiter placed steaming plates of pasta in front of them. "Now, let's dig in before our food gets cold."

Abby grinned. "I'll start the research, and when I'm ready, we can talk."

"Let's change the subject." Shane steered the conversation to other topics, such as vacation spots, favorite movies, and anything else that could pop up.

The conversation didn't slow as they drove to the movie. While they waited for it to start she said, "I can't believe this is the first time I've been to a drive-in!" Abby took in the surrounding activity as darkened parking spaces filled in around them.

Shane was enjoying his date. The movies were secondary compared to spending the evening alone with Abby.

"Let's take a walk before the movie starts and get some popcorn and drinks."

She looked at him. "You're kidding. You have room for popcorn?"

"I didn't say we had to eat it, but I think you can't go to a drive-in without getting a box." He chuckled. "I think there is an unwritten law somewhere; popcorn, candy, and drinks must be purchased."

"I don't see the snack stand?"

Shane pointed to a small mound jutting from the ground at the edge of the screen. "See that? It's built into the side of the hill. It prevents the lights from the concession stand from spoiling the viewing area."

They wandered around the grassy parking lot holding hands. After buying too much of everything, they made their way back to the truck. The moon illuminated the night sky, and stars dusted the inky backdrop. Opening credits rolled over the screen and Abby snuggled into the circle of Shane's arm. He pulled her close, nuzzling her neck, his breath tickling the base of her throat. When goose bumps raced down her arms, he smoothed them away with the heat of his hand.

"We're acting like a couple of teenagers," she whispered.

"I never did this at a drive-in. It's okay; we're regressing." He spoke softly in her ear.

"We should be watching the movie," Abby giggled softly.

"I'm not a big fan of cartoons." His lips continued their deliciously slow journey.

Abby shivered, her resistance weakening. "Shane."

"Hmm?" he continued to caress her neck. "Do you want me to stop?"

Words forgotten, she turned and melted into him. Tentatively with a brush of lips, his desire grew in intensity. He had never before been kissed, not like this, with such tenderness, passion, and longing for more, much more.

"Do you want to go someplace more private?" Shane hoped she would say yes.

Abby tilted her head with a saucy grin. "Can I have a rain check on the movie?"

"Rain check issued," Shane simply stated.

Abby swallowed her nerves. "Take me home and stay."

21

---

*T*he drive to Abby's house flew by. Few words were exchanged. They held tight to each other's hands. Shane pulled in the driveway, threw the truck in park, and turned off the engine. Slowly, he turned to her, looking deep into her smoky gray eyes.

"I will ask you this one time. Are you sure you want me to come in? If not, I understand, and I'll see you tomorrow." Shane waited, his blood pounding in his veins.

She held up their clasped hands. "Stay with me," she whispered.

"For as long as you want," he murmured.

She slid across the seat into his open arms. He held her close, savoring the moonlit moment. Abby led the way to the back door. Chivalrously, he took the key and pushed the door open, allowing her to enter ahead of him.

A solitary light welcomed them into the silent house. Without a word, Abby glided up the darkened staircase. He followed. The bedroom door stood open, and moonlight bathed the room in a soft glow. Through the open windows, the scent of the Casablanca lily hovered in the warm night air. Abby crossed the room to turn on a small table lamp.

He was a step behind her and clicked it off. "The moonlight is perfect," he said in a low voice.

*H*e stretched out his hand to Abby, guiding her to his chest. She lightly placed her hand in his as a tremor shot through her. He grazed her delicate jawline as she quivered in response.

He lowered his brow to hers. "Let's take our time," Shane spoke just above a whisper.

She was baffled. Maybe he sensed her lack of skills in the art of lovemaking.

He continued to run his fingers over her heart-shaped face. "We have all night."

She gave into the sensations that were rippling over her. Shane's fingers trailed the outline of her eyes, down her nose, gliding over cheeks to gently caress her collarbone. His lips followed the same path, leaving a trail of lingering heat as he awakened unknown needs and desires deep inside her. He eased her back onto the soft bed. Her nerves gave way to pleasure. Involuntarily, she groaned as his hands slid down from her shoulders, skimming the soft skin in the crook of her arm. Abby had never experienced the sensations that threatened to overtake her.

If he felt her hesitancy he moved slowly to explore every exposed inch of her. This night was magical.

She moaned as his tongue played over her lips. She met his mouth with a deep, demanding kiss. Passion overruled caution, and she ripped at his shirt, freeing it from his body, allowing her to toss it aside. Her fingers traveled the broad expanse of his back, following the curve of his spine. He groaned, pressing his body into her soft, yielding form. Shane was under her spell.

He let Abby set the rhythm. Her pulse quickened and blood hummed in her veins.

Time was lost as she gave into the rolling sensations. This was like a novel she had read; the hero and heroine lost in each other's arms, oblivious to the world outside the bedroom door. She arched into him. It was the invitation Shane seemed to need.

He slid a calloused hand under her shirt. Abby shuddered as his finger toyed with the lace on her bra, following the outline of her breast. He slid his thumb over the satin-covered nipple. She writhed under his touch. She guided his hand to the front clasp. Quickly, he snapped it open, pushing it back to expose soft white mounds beneath his hands.

"My shirt," Abby said breathlessly.

In one fluid motion, he pulled off her shirt and bra, leaving her bathed in soft light of the moon. His mouth played with a newly exposed nipple until it stood hard and erect. His teeth lightly grazed it, teasing until her body arched in response and the fire under her skin overcame her. She pulled his mouth to hers to sear his lips with the heat that poured from her soul.

"I want to feel all of you," Abby demanded.

Shane smoothly helped Abby out of her jeans and sandals.

Nerves long forgotten, Abby said with a sultry laugh, "Shall I help you?"

"Next time, love." He pulled off his jeans and lay down next to her, determined to take things slow despite the overwhelming passion that drove them.

Abby slipped her hand down to the center of this kind

and gentle man, finding him hard and ready. Self-doubt crept in. She remembered that she had been told by her first and only serious boyfriend that she was a cold fish. She pushed the painful memory aside, determined to enjoy this time with Shane, even if it was only for one night. She slid on top of him, wanting to feel his skin against hers.

He groaned. "You're torturing me with your mouth and body."

"Protection?" she questioned. This wasn't the time to be irresponsible.

"Yes." Shane's lips brushed over hers as he retrieved a small packet from his jeans pocket. He held it up in triumph. "Are you ready? We can slow this down."

Abby shook her head. "Almost. But first I have to tell you something." She swallowed the tears that threatened to spill.

Holding her tightly, gently he said, "You can tell me anything."

She took a deep breath, briefly hesitating, and said, "I've never done this before."

He was taken aback. Not sure what to say next, he paused. "Are you sure you want to, you know, do this? We can stop right now."

"I've waited for the right moment, and I want it to be tonight with you." She covered his mouth with hers.

He pulled her close, at first moving cautiously, then matching her kiss for kiss, stroke for stroke, heat devouring them both. Shane's hands roamed freely over her heat scorched skin, sliding down until he reached her soft center. He rubbed his thumb over the sensitive spot, and immediately she sighed. Like the night flower blooming under the moonlight, Abby opened herself to him. He gently slid into her, moving slowly so as not to cause her discomfort. She arched into him, wrapping her legs tight, pulling him closer. They moved in perfect rhythm, pushing each other higher and higher until Abby cried out with release. Shane slowed until the peak passed. She drew in deep ragged breaths and moved under him. His eyes met hers as his needs engulfed him. Her movements urged him to bring them to a new high. Unable to hold back any longer, he let go as she cried out, his orgasm crashing over her like ocean waves.

Bathed in a sheen of sweat, they lay in each other's arms, gasping for breath.

She felt the tears slip from the corners of her eyes. It was the single most glorious experience of her adult life. Her only regret she was sorry that she couldn't help him reach the same heights.

"Shane?"

Unable to speak he uttered, "Um?"

With a catch in her voice, she said, "I'm sorry."

"Sorry? For what?"

"That I'm a cold fish and inexperienced…" she began.

"What are you talking about?" he said, half amused.

She started to cry. "You don't have to pretend that you…"

Shocked that she was serious, he cradled her in his arms. "Abby, in case you missed it, you blew me away." He brushed his lips over her hair and gently stroked her hand. "Being with you tonight taught me what it's like to have a relationship with many layers. I may sound like a sap, but I feel this was the first time for me too."

"Shane, that is the sweetest thing you could have said," she sniffled.

He put his finger under her chin and lifted her face to

be a breath away from his. "Abby, tonight I wanted to show you how I feel about you. It's the feelings we have for each other that made this night so incredible."

Using his thumb, Shane wiped the tears from her face.

At a loss for words, Abby kissed him, covering his mouth, face, and neck with her lips.

"Do you know where this will lead?" he asked in a deep, husky voice.

She grinned in the moonlight. "Yes, I do."

*a*bby found herself wrapped around a tall, lanky naked man. The sun was streaming over the rumpled bed. Lying still, she listened to him lightly snoring. She attempted, in vain, to peek at the clock to check the time but the weight of his body kept her a happy hostage. Basking in the glow of the last twelve hours, she couldn't help but smile to herself.

Shane opened one eye and squinted. "I guess we forgot to close the blinds," he grumbled. Rubbing his eyes, Shane looked at Abby. "Good morning," he said, wearing a crooked smile.

A shy smiled crept over her face. "Did you sleep well?"

"Like a rock, you?" He rolled over to face her, adjusting his arms so he could pull her close.

She dragged the sheet over them. "Never better."

He brushed his lips to hers—lingering, teasing, and tasting, pausing long enough to ask, "What do you want to do today?"

"I told Kate I'd pick Devin up around noon and then we're going to the lake. You're welcome to come along if you'd like." Abby didn't think Shane was ready for a day filled with her and the baby.

"Sounds like a plan. We'll meet everyone at my place," he said as he nuzzled her neck, working his way down her body. "What time are we picking up the little guy?" he mumbled.

Abby sighed as her head began to spin and her body quivered. "We have plenty of time."

*K*ate glanced out the kitchen window to discover her brother and Abby strolling up the driveway, hand in hand and grinning. Something had definitely changed between the couple.

"Don, quick. Take a look."

Her peered over her shoulder. "They suit each other, Katie." He squeezed her arm and bussed her cheek. "We shouldn't get caught being Peeping Toms." He pulled her from the window. "Why don't you go get Devin, and I'll get the door."

Don swung the door open wide and held back a grin. "Well, hello you two. How was the drive-in?"

"We had a wonderful evening, thank you." Abby tried to be cool but burst into laughter. "The restaurant was great; the drive-in was so much fun. I hope we can go back again, and soon." Abby gave Shane a knowing smile.

He kept his poker face steady and turned the questions back on his sister and her husband. "How was the little guy last night?"

Kate came around the corner carrying the baby. "Devin was an angel. We put him down, and he didn't wake up until about seven. We've had a busy morning. He and Don have spent the majority of the time playing trucks, so he might need a nap soon. The boys had just settled on the couch before you got here."

She breathed a sigh of relief. "That's good to hear. I wasn't sure how he would do in a strange house. I should have known he would be fine. He's become attached to both of you. Kate, I told Shane we're going to the lake, and he's volunteered his personal beach for us to while the afternoon away."

"Sounds like a party is brewing to me," Don stated.

Kate agreed. "I should call Ellie; I'm sure she could use a break from studying."

Abby bent to pick up the baby. "Of course. The more, the merrier, if that's okay with you." She looked up at Shane. She spent a great deal of time alone; time with her friends was precious.

"Ask her to call Mom and Ray. We can throw together a potluck picnic, and I'll call Jake."

Shane moved out of earshot. He answered with a quick hello. Before Shane told him that everyone was getting together at the lake, he blurted out, "I got it, man. I'm never letting her go."

Jake shouted, "Yes! So, when's the wedding, bro?"

"I'm going to wait until everything is settled with Devin and then I'm popping the question. I'm also going to ask her to let the three of us be a real family. I want to adopt Devin and raise him as my son. Jake, the boy needs a dad, not just an uncle."

"Yeah, I hear ya. Abby and Devin are going to fill your life with more happiness than you could imagine."

He choked up. "Hey, we're going out to my place this

afternoon. The family is pulling together a cookout. If you and Sara are up for it, come on out, even if it's for a little while. There are plenty of hands to play pass the baby."

"Let me run it by Sara. But no guarantees, it'll depend on the kids. We're trying to get them into some sort of a routine. Everyone's been great pitching in and helping, but at some point, we have to manage them on our own."

"Isn't that why we have family?" Shane joked.

"We are going to have a lot of favors to repay."

"You'd do the same for any of us, so chill out. Someday, maybe I'll have triplets, and you can change diapers." He surprised himself, talking about having more children when he had just announced he intended to adopt Devin. He hadn't pictured his future with a wife, let alone children. How fast things change, he mused.

"Alright, well, I've got babies to tend to. I'll catch you later." Jake hung up as a tiny wail came through the phone.

Shane went back toward the house to see Don lugging baby stuff out to Abby's SUV. Kate and Abby finished gathering up Devin's toys and extra clothes. He overheard the girls talking about what was needed from the grocery store, and Kate said she'd take care of the list.

She hugged Kate tightly and whispered in her ear, "I'm in serious like with your brother."

Kate admonished in a whisper, "'Like,' Abby? Are you sure that's all it is?"

Kate picked up the diaper bag and handed it to Shane. "See you in a while, big brother." She hugged Abby and Devin and watched as the three of them got ready to leave.

Shane slid behind the steering wheel. "Do we need to stop at your place?"

"Yes, I need to get a few extra things for Devin, and I want to swing by the market. I'd like to make a couple of things for the cookout. Kate and Cari are going to bring the rest."

"Your wish is my command." Before pulling away from the curb, Shane gave her a quick kiss.

Kate and Don stood on the step, watching them drive off. "I think wedding bells are going to ring soon." She squeezed his hand. "I'm so happy for all of them."

"It's been a long time coming for Shane. I don't think he could do any better. Abby is a great girl and Devin completes the package." He placed a tender kiss on Kate's brow. "Our day is coming, sweetheart. Soon, we'll expand our family."

A lone tear slid down Kate's cheek. "Don, I pray you're right."

By midafternoon, the entire McKenna-Davis family had gathered at the lake house. There were three porta cribs in the master bedroom, and a baby monitor rested on the picnic table. For a new mother, Sara looked amazingly well rested. Meanwhile, Jake was vigilant about checking on the babies.

The family enjoyed a fun day under the brilliant blue sky. As darkness fell, the party broke up. Abby took a few things to her vehicle and realized Shane's truck was still at her place.

"You should have driven your truck instead of driving us."

"Well, I was thinking I could go home with you tonight." He didn't seem to be ready for the day to be over.

"Devin wakes up early every day; he doesn't understand the concept of a weekend."

"That's fine; it just gives me more time to spend with both of you." He leaned in for a quick peck on her lips.

Abby sighed. Everything but the kiss drifted away as she wrapped her arms around his waist. Devin took the opportunity to start chattering loudly from his stroller.

Reluctantly, he released Abby.

"Do you want smooches, babycakes?" She unbuckled him. "Are you ready to go home?"

Devin happily patted her cheeks, smearing them with cookie crumbs.

"Devin, I think bath and bed are coming up next." Abby looked at Shane, and he nodded. It was time to head into town. This was new territory for both of them. But he seemed to be adjusting to it quickly.

"I'll get the rest of his stuff, and we can go. If it would help, I can sit in the back and keep Devin awake until we get back to your place?" Shane volunteered.

"Good idea. If you lightly tickle his feet, that will keep him awake. Once he falls asleep, he'll be out for the night."

After all the rest of the stuff was loaded in the back Shane settled in the back seat. "Ready to go home, buddy?"

Devin looked up and gave him a sleepy smile. "Abs, he's ready to conk out; we'd better get going."

She glanced in the rearview mirror. Her heart warmed.

For the first time in a very long time, she felt like life was going to be okay.

*S*hane's eyes met Abby's. A new feeling warmed his heart. After the final custody hearing was behind them, he was going to make this woman his wife, and together with this little boy, they would become a family.

23

_D_on noticed Shane had been unusually quiet during the previous few days. The weight of the world seemed to be on his shoulders. Not one to pry, he waited for Shane to feel ready to get off his chest whatever was bugging him. His behavior was out of character, even more so because it was just this past weekend when everyone had gotten together, and Shane had seemed to be walking on air, having decided he wanted Abby and Devin to become a significant part of his life. Don had mentioned Shane's mood to Kate, and she agreed that patience was the best course of action.

_A_fter a few more days had passed in silence, Shane couldn't think straight. "Don, can I talk to you about something, but don't say anything to Kate?"

"Shoot."

Shane stopped the truck in the parking lot of the tree nursery. He drummed his fingers on the steering wheel and said, "I'm not sure if I'm doing the right thing for the right reasons."

"What are you talking about? I need a few more details if you want advice."

"You know I've been spending a lot of time with Abby and Devin." Shane stopped and stared out the window. "I feel like a real jerk. I don't know if I'm ready for an instant family."

Don, never one to be accused of being talkative, waited for Shane to continue.

"I never thought I'd have kids or get married. Abby is great, and Devin is amazing. If it was just Abby, I'd be all in, but Devin adds a layer of complication. His grandparents are always calling and checking up on them. They have Abby on a short leash. Do I really want to live my life answering to them?"

"Sounds like you're getting cold feet. It's normal."

"I think I'm going to put some space between me and Abby. Yup, I'm going to take a breather and find a way to break it off before either of us gets any more invested and then she ends up getting hurt." Satisfied with his decision, he moved to get out of the truck. "You coming?"

Don looked at Shane. "Are you sure you want to break it off with her?"

"I don't want to, but I don't have a choice. I'm not ready to be a full-time parent. Someday, she'll thank me for being honest."

"Man, have you seen how she looks at you? I don't think she'll ever thank you for breaking her heart 'cause that girl is head over heels for you. If you want my honest opinion, Shane, you're a damn fool."

Don got out of the truck, slammed the door, and headed to the office.

He was glued to the seat. Was he being stupid? Was walking away from Abby and Devin something he would regret? Only time could give him the answers to the questions crowding his thoughts.

*

*A*bby sat at the desk in Shane's office, deep in thought. Something was different between them, but she couldn't put her finger on what had happened. They had been spending a lot of time together; they'd had a romantic date that led to an amazing weekend. But the last couple of days, Shane seemed to be making excuses to leave her house early, and he wasn't calling the office as much just to say hello. Maybe she was being overly sensitive. With everything going on in her life, she didn't expect anything to run smoothly. Her cell phone rang, jarring her back to the present.

"Hello," she spoke quietly.

"Abigail, Edward Martin here."

"Hello, Edward. How can I help you today?" Abby sighed. Would these calls ever stop? She wondered.

"I wanted to make sure that my grandson is doing well today."

"Edward, Devin is currently napping, but I can assure you he is thriving. I'm sure you received a copy of his most recent visit to the pediatrician."

"Yes. I received that yesterday, and that is why I'm calling. I wanted to thank you for keeping Mrs. Martin and myself up-to-date. Well, have a good day, and I will talk with you tomorrow." Abruptly, he disconnected.

Abby stared at the phone in her hand. Despite her irritation, she was happy that she had thought to send them a copy of the baby's records. Complete transparency would hopefully be a point in her favor with the court. She turned the short conversation over in her head. "Hmm, he told me to have a good day. Could it be he is starting to realize Devin is loved and that I put his needs first?" she said to herself. But then, chiding herself for dreaming an impossible dream, she went back to work.

*

*A*bby was finishing the salad when Shane knocked on the back door. Without waiting for her to open it, he came inside.

"Hey, Abs. I don't think I can stay for dinner tonight. I need to go look at a new job over in Everett. It could be a good one for us if I can get a good idea of the scope of work and create a competitive quote. I'll leave information on your desk and maybe you could get the price quote done first thing tomorrow. I want to be the first quote in, and it might give us an edge over the competition." Shane paused as he noticed the table was set for the two of them. Feeling like a jerk, he said, "I'm sorry, Abby. I should have called earlier."

He hoped his reason for skipping out on dinner would sound plausible. But if he was being truthful, he couldn't bear to see Abby and hold his ground that he was going to break off their budding relationship.

*A*bby couldn't believe her ears. She wasn't stupid; he *was* avoiding her, and she was going to find out why. "You're right. You should have called. But no worries, I can put most of this in the freezer for another time." She turned her back on Shane, took a deep breath, and squared her shoulders before facing him. "Before you go, can we talk about what is bothering you?"

"I'm not sure what you're talking about. Nothing is bothering me other than the fact that I have the chance to bid on a big job that will carry the crew for at least a month." Shane avoided looking her in the eye.

"Please, give me a couple of minutes." She gestured to a chair. "Will you sit down?"

He dragged the chair over the tile floor and did as she requested. He waited for her to start.

"Shane, for the last several days, I've noticed you've been creating distance between us, not just physically but in our conversations too. What is going on? Are you having second thoughts about a relationship with me?" A lump stuck in Abby's throat as she spoke the words she feared.

"Ah, Abs. It's not what you think." He was immediately sorry for what he was about to say. "I never saw myself getting married and having a family. I thought I'd be the fun bachelor uncle, having a good time and enjoying life."

"Shane, I'm not asking you to marry me." A storm was gathering in her eyes, and Shane jumped in, heedless of the warning signs.

"I know you haven't said anything about getting married. But it's what you deserve, Abby. You are the kind of girl who would make some guy really lucky to have you as a wife." Unaware he was making things worse than they started out, he kept rambling on. "If circumstances were different, we could go on having a great time. But I have to be an adult and think about Devin." He stopped, struck by the look that was frozen on Abby's face.

She pushed back her chair and pointed to the door. "Get out of my house." Without another word, she left the kitchen.

*S*tunned, he slowly stood, wondering if he should go after her. He listened to her talking in soft tones to Devin and then he heard her say, "We're going to be fine, Devin. It will always be just the two of us. We don't need anyone else."

With a heavy heart, Shane knew he was no longer welcome and walked out the door and out of Abby and Devin's lives.

*S*he heard the truck roar to life, and a trickle of tears released into a river. Great sobs ripped her heart, and she clung to Devin.

After allowing herself a few minutes to cry, she put him on the floor to play, dried her face, and sat down to figure out where everything took a wrong turn. She heard her cell blip with a text message. She made sure Devin was occupied and then went to see who had texted.

I'm sorry. I want us to be friends, and I hope you still want to work for me. If you don't, I understand. Just let me know.

*S*he flung the phone into her handbag and went back to the living room. How dare he think she would quit her job! It was something she enjoyed. She would be professional and continue to work for McKenna Landscaping.

✦

*C*ari went into the kitchen at What's Perkin' where Kate was scooping batter into muffin tins. "Have you talked to Abby lately? She hasn't been in for lunch or coffee since before last weekend."

"Now that you mention it, no, and that is strange. I'll give her a call and see what's going on and ask her to come by for lunch today."

Kate dialed the phone. "It went to voicemail. I'll call the office phone. Maybe she left her cell in the car."

After several rings, Abby picked up. "McKenna Landscaping. This is Abby, may I help you?"

"Yes, you can." Kate smiled into the phone. "There's an empty chair in the shop. Care to join us?"

"Jeez, Kate. I can't today. I have a ton of work here, and I need to get home early and get some stuff done there. But thanks for the call. I'll talk to you later." Abby hung up.

Kate turned to her mother. "Something's up. Abby couldn't wait to get off the phone. If she doesn't stop in tomorrow, I'll drop by her house and do some snooping. I didn't like the tone in her voice."

Cari agreed with Kate. Abby was alone, and this wasn't a good time for her to withdraw from everyone. The stress she was under from the custody battle was likely overwhelming. She made a mental note to give Shane a call after work and see if he had any idea what was going on with her.

Cari left a message on Shane's cell and asked him to call or swing by the house that night. She didn't mention anything more but was sure he would be in touch. It didn't take long before he called and said he'd stop by around dinner. She asked if he'd like to join her and Ray, which he quickly agreed to do.

She was on the back deck, enjoying a few minutes of quiet when Shane arrived. She shot him a warm smile and waved him up to the deck.

"Hello, son. If you'd like something to drink, help yourself. My feet are so tired. We were busy all day."

Shane leaned down and gave his mother a peck on the cheek. "Okay, be right back." Shane looked at her half-empty glass of iced tea. "Do you need a refill?"

"That would be lovely. Thank you." She passed him the glass and leaned back in her chair.

He went inside and reappeared shortly. Shane handed a full glass to his mother and sat down next to her, stretching out his long legs. "Where's Ray?"

"He called and said he needed to finish up something on the job he's doing. He'll be home in about an hour. I told him you were stopping by and we'd have dinner when he got home." Cari studied her oldest child. She could see something was amiss. "So, do you want to talk about it?"

Shane reclined in his chair with his eyes closed. "Talk about what?"

"Whatever has given you the weight of the world on your shoulders. I have a feeling it has something to do with a certain young lady and a little boy."

He shifted uncomfortably under his mother's gaze. He decided to get it over with. "We broke up."

Cari sat up straight. "What do you mean, you and Abby broke up? I've seen the two of you together, and I've seen you with Devin. You are perfect for each other."

"Mom, it's simple. Abby and Devin need someone who can be there for them and deal with the Martin's. They're never going to leave her alone, and I don't want my life to be under that kind of a microscope. I thought it best to break it off now rather than let everyone get really attached and then let them down later. It's better this way for all of us."

Her temper spiked. "Really, you thought it best? Was Abby pressuring you for a commitment to her and Devin? Did she ever say that she expected you to be her white knight and save her from the evil Martin's?" Cari didn't attempt to hide her irritation from her son.

"Abby never suggested anything of the sort. It was all me. After the weekend, I gave it a lot of thought and knew I couldn't give her what she deserved. So, the other night we had a talk, and I told her that we should be friends."

She stared at him. She was dumbfounded. Minutes ticked by before she could think of something to say to her son. She didn't want to mince words. "Shane. For the first time in a very long time, I have to tell you that I am very disappointed." She let the words penetrate his thick skull. "You didn't break up with Abby so that she could find someone who was right for her; you broke it off because you are scared of the intense feelings you have for her and Devin."

Shane started to protest, and Cari cut him off. "Face it; you're out of your comfort zone, and you have no idea how to handle these feelings. You had better think long and hard before too much time passes and you lose your chance with Abby forever. Remember, I saw the two of you together, and a blind man could see how you feel about each other. The connection you share is a gift, Shane."

. . .

*H*e didn't look at his mother. For the first time in his life, he wanted to cry over a girl. Had he pushed Abby away because he didn't know how to handle the feelings that threatened to overwhelm him? Maybe his mom was right, and he'd better give this some more thought.

Mother and son sat in the late afternoon sun in silence. There was nothing left to say.

"Mom, I'm going to head home. I'll catch dinner with you and Ray some other night. I have some thinking to do. You may be right, and if Abby is the woman I'm supposed to be with, I'd better figure it out." Shane dropped a kiss on the top of Mom's head and walked with a heavy heart to his truck.

*C*ari was still sitting on the deck when Ray got home. "Where's Shane? I thought he was going to have dinner with us." Ray kissed his wife and sat next to her.

With a wave of her hand she said, "Shane broke it off with Abby. We had a long talk and then he went home to give it some more thought. In a nutshell, he's scared of his feelings. He's never felt like this before, and instead of facing it, he ran. Hopefully, he'll do some soul searching, then call her and make things right between them." Cari looked at her husband, her eyes shining with happiness. "I am so lucky that we found each other. All I want is for our kids to be as happy as we are."

"Sweetheart, Shane will figure it out. We did." Ray took Cari's hand in his and gave it a kiss.

"You're right. I just don't want Abby and Shane to take fifteen years to figure it out." She gave a small laugh and said, "But I guess everything in its own time."

Ray chuckled. "Thank heaven we did." Ray helped Cari up and into his welcoming arms. "Let's go make some dinner, and who knows where the rest of the night will go."

"I like the way you think, Mr. Davis."

*a*bby's house phone was ringing incessantly as she pulled the diaper bag off the stroller's handles. She glanced at Devin, who was happily gumming a cookie, as she reached for the phone. Breathless, she said, "Hello?"

"Abby? Kyle Baird. How are you?"

"Fine, thank you." Abby was taken aback by his businesslike tone.

"I wanted to let you know we have to be in court Tuesday at nine."

She sagged against the counter. "I'll be there. Should I bring the baby with me? I'm sure I can get someone to take care of him while we see the judge."

"I think that would be for the best. Judge Roy may want to see him. I understand the Martin's haven't seen him, as they refused supervised visitation." Kyle stated the facts as he knew them.

"They've been in touch by phone daily. I understand they weren't comfortable with supervised visitation, so they declined."

"Interesting."

Abby waited for Kyle to expand on his comment.

I'll meet you at the courthouse. We should be done by noon, and soon this will be a part of the past." Kyle disconnected and swiveled around in his chair to stare out the window.

Kyle had done his best to reassure Abby, but he wasn't sure which way the judge would rule. The Martin's had a lot of influence in the community, and he knew the home visits had gone smoothly. However, Abby did have a few things going for her, and Kyle intended, if necessary, to reiterate them.

But the real game changer would be the letter Tim and Kelly had drafted and Kyle notarized. Only three people knew the contents—well, now four since Judge Roy received a copy. Devin Martin belonged with his aunt, Abigail Stevens, and Kyle planned to do everything he could to honor his friend's request.

🍷

*S*hane knocked on the back door. He could see through the screen that Abby was feeding the baby. Her eyes lit up when she saw him. "Hello there. I'm surprised to see you."

"Hello, yourself. Can we talk?" He bent low to tickle Devin under his chin.

Abby hesitated. "Sure."

Shane pulled out a chair and sat at the table. He kept his hands occupied by twirling his sunglasses. He wasn't sure where to begin. "I had a long talk with my mom a couple of nights ago. And in typical mom fashion, she pointed out that I should stop being scared of the future I could have and wake up before I blew it altogether."

Abby looked at him, confusion filled her eyes. "I don't understand. Why are you here?"

"The other day, when I came over and basically broke things off, I didn't mean it. I'm crazy about you and Devin. I don't want to lose either of you. I have no idea how to be a real boyfriend since I've never had a long-term relationship, but if you can be patient and give me a chance, I want to be yours. That's if you can forgive me for hurting you."

She didn't respond. She moved around the kitchen, picking things up and putting them down, and then grabbed a washcloth to wipe Devin's face and hands. Silence hung heavy in the late afternoon air.

He stood up. He had overstayed his welcome. He gently touched her hand as he turned to leave.

"Kyle Baird called today. I have to drive to Boston next week. We have a court date Tuesday at nine."

Shane stopped mid-step. "That means this will be over soon. I'm happy for you."

"I was thinking of going out there Monday night. I would hate to be late for court, and you never know about traffic. I'm going to ask Cari if she'll go with me. Kyle suggested I have someone look after Devin while we're in with the judge."

"I'm sure she'll be happy to help. You should give her a call after dinner."

She looked him square in the eyes. "Shane, I know there's a lot going on at work, but if you were interested in coming with us, I'd love to have the support."

Shane pulled her into his arms and locked his gaze on

hers. "I'm not running anymore, Abs. We started this together, and we'll finish it. Together."

"I'm still not sure what caused you to bolt. I'm not going to dwell on it, but I do want to talk about this after I've put Devin down for the night. I have enough to worry about, and I'd like to understand what happened. But I'm relieved you want to go with us. I feel like David going to meet Goliath." Abby squeezed Shane hard before letting go.

"Dinner?" she asked.

Devin started to jabber, waving his little hands in the air.

"And someone is looking for attention," she added.

"I've got him." Shane turned to Devin. "Would you like to get out of there?"

Devin wiggled in his high chair, squealing in delight. Happy to oblige, Shane pulled him out and took him to the sink. "I think he needs to be hosed off. What did you feed him tonight?"

Abby didn't hear his question because she was deep in thought. "Shane, for the last several weeks, I've been thinking. I've decided that once the custody issue is settled, I want to adopt Devin. I'm going to talk to Kyle about legally adopting him. That way, no one can ever try to take him from me again."

"I think it's a really good idea, for Devin and for you. You're the only mother he is going to remember. If he were older, it would be different. Talk to Kyle and consider the pros and cons." Shane looked directly into Abby's eyes. "How do you think the Martin's will react?"

"Honestly, I'm sure they'll want to fight me. I'm going to keep his last name Martin and lock up his trust fund until he's ready for college. I can't think of any reason for them to object. But I could be wrong."

*A*bby shrugged her shoulders and turned to the stove. She would make sure that Devin knew exactly who his parents were and how much he was loved. She was going to call Kyle Baird in the morning. If it was possible, maybe they could get the paperwork started next week.

"Shane, after dinner let's take a walk down for ice cream and hang out in the park, just for a while? The weather is perfect, and I could use a distraction, and maybe we can continue our conversation about your recent bout of cold feet."

"Devin loves the park, and I'd like to continue our talk. I'm sure you have more to say." With a wicked gleam in his eye, he said, "Better yet, let's skip dinner and go for a double scoop. We can work off the extra calories while we walk."

Abby pretended to look shocked but quickly dissolved into laughter.

"I'll get the stroller, and you change the baby."

"Wait," Shane sputtered. "How did I get diaper duty?"

Abby's laughter drifted to him, and he smiled despite the smell coming from the angel-faced baby. "Come on, stinky pants. Let's get you ready for an evening on the town."

A few minutes before nine o'clock, Shane stood next to Abby on the courthouse steps. Kyle arrived, nodding with approval at their attire, and asked, "Where is Devin?"

"He was getting fussy sitting still, so Shane's parents, Cari and Ray, took him for a walk," Abby explained. "They'll be back shortly. I asked them to meet us inside."

"Good. We should go in and get set up. I'm assuming the Martin's are inside. I have copies of the reports from the accountant and Noreen Landry, just in case there has been a paperwork snafu. I'm not taking any chances today."

Abby clung to Shane's hand as they climbed the wide stone steps. Making a point to wear formal business attire, Shane had donned a dark gray pinstripe suit with a deep blue tie. Abby had chosen a skirt and jacket combination from her former working life.

They entered the courtroom, which was nearly empty save for the Martin's and their lawyer, who were settled at a conference table in front of the judge's bench. Kyle gestured to the table across the aisle from them, indicating Abby should take a seat. Shane sat behind them. Edward and Louise Martin were expressionless. Edward surveyed the room. He leaned toward his lawyer, speaking in hushed tones. The lawyer did a half turn in his chair and held up a hand, indicating Edward needed to be quiet.

Abby was watching the exchange when she heard the door in the back of the courtroom open. Abby turned, expecting to see Cari and Ray with Devin. To her surprise, Shane's family, everyone except for Sara, strode into the courtroom with Ray leading the way and pushing Devin in the stroller. Abby was speechless. Quickly, everyone took a seat just as Judge Roy made her entrance.

Edward flashed a look of contempt in Abby's direction.

"All rise, for the Honorable Judge Roy," commanded the bailiff.

The judge took her place at the large desk, which dominated the room.

The bailiff turned to address the group. "Be seated and come to order."

Out of the corner of her eye, Abby saw Devin making the rounds, giving sloppy kisses to each member of the McKenna-Davis family.

*J*udge Roy observed him interacting with the group sitting behind Abby. She took a few moments to study the papers in front of her before addressing Abby, Edward, and Louise.

"Well, it's been a while since we were all together." Judge Roy wanted to keep this exchange friendly. In similar cases, she had found this strategy to be in the best interest of the child.

"I see the little boy is in the courtroom today. He seems to be enjoying himself back there. Mr. Baird, I believe I'm going to be a little unorthodox today. I'd like to ask a few questions and, given these circumstances, I feel it is appropriate to make myself aware of certain facts before I announce my decision."

Kyle stood to address her. "Of course, ma'am."

"Ms. Stevens, I see you have been visited, several times, by Noreen Landry from Social Services. She has spoken highly of your home and place of employment.

I've also reviewed the reports from the pediatrician and all the financial records we requested from you. I would like to commend you on your willingness to provide anything the court has requested. Thank you."

Judge Roy turned her attention to the Martin's.

"Mr. and Mrs. Martin, I see that you have also given Social Services complete access to your home. But I see in the notes that since the last time we met, you waived your right to supervised visitation and have been in contact with Ms. Stevens exclusively via telephone." She paused, flipping through the file. "I see you have been calling at various times throughout each day. It seems you've been checking up on her. Did you expect she would follow your example and leave the state?"

Edward became red in the face and jabbed the air in his lawyer's direction.

She looked down at him, waiting for a response. "No need to answer that."

"Your Honor. May I address the court?" The Martin's lawyer stood up.

"And you are? Mister...?" she inquired. "I don't believe you were at our last emergency meeting."

"I'm sorry, Your Honor. I'm Robert Jones. I'm here today to represent Mr. and Mrs. Martin."

The judge patiently waited for him to continue.

"Both Mr. and Mrs. Martin were insulted that the court would order supervised visitation with their grandson, which is why they chose not to see him during that time. They didn't want to spend time in the company of Abigail Stevens, who they feel is not suitable to raise their only grandson."

Judge Roy removed her reading glasses and turned her full attention to the Martin's.

"Well, it is up to me to determine who is a suitable guardian for the child based on evidence and experience. Of which I might add, I have both, and that includes a sealed letter from Timothy and Kelly Martin."

Edward grabbed his lawyer's arm. "What is she talking about? What is that little good-for-nothing gold digger trying to pull now?"

Robert Jones pulled his arm away. "Quiet," he hissed. "I'm sure the judge will tell us." He turned to address the judge. "I'm sorry, Your Honor, for Mr. Martin's outburst. I'm sure you can understand that this is very emotional for him."

Judge Roy looked at Edward while directing her comment to Mr. Jones. "Please remind your client that this is my courtroom and I will not tolerate such derogatory comments about anyone. This is his only and final warning. Do I make myself clear?"

"Of course, Your Honor. We were surprised. Neither myself nor Mr. Martin knew anything about another letter from his son. Is this the same letter that Mr. Martin was given by Mr. Baird?"

The judge didn't respond to the question that hung in the air. She turned her attention to Abby. "Ms. Stevens, I would like to ask you a couple of questions."

*A*bby stood up, knees knocking so much that she had to rest her hands on the table for support. "Yes, ma'am," she said very softly.

"Would you introduce me to the people who are sitting with Devin?"

Taken aback, she stammered, "Of course, Your Honor."

One by one, Abby introduced everyone, giving a brief background of how long she had known each of them.

"These people are Devin's and my family. We're very blessed to have them in our lives."

The judge had been observing the baby's rapport with the group.

"Well, it seems to me the minor child is well cared for, his basic needs are more than being met, but more importantly, he is being raised with people who obviously love him a great deal."

Judge Roy gave the Martin's a stern look. "Mr. Martin, Mrs. Martin, do you disagree that your grandson's welfare is the most important factor in this proceeding?"

Edward slowly nodded his head, unsure if he should speak.

"Good. I'm glad we're on the same page. I have been shown nothing that would cause me to have concern for this child, other than when you decided to leave town without telling his guardian of your intentions. My ruling is to grant full physical and legal custody to Abigail Stevens."

"Wait!" Edward demanded.

Before pounding the gavel, she gave Edward a withering look, which made him and Louise shrink in their chairs. "Excuse me?"

"You mentioned a letter from my son? I demand to know the contents." Edward's face had turned an alarming shade of purple.

"I'm happy to provide a copy to your lawyer. Suffice it to say that your son and his wife anticipated you would challenge their request and, in the letter, stated the explicit reason why Ms. Stevens is the best choice to raise their son. I admit the circumstances have been a little unusual, but their intent was clear. To put it simply, your son wanted his son raised without the constraints that you placed on him as a child."

Edward and Louise cowered under the commanding voice of the judge, who waited for a response. A pin drop could have been heard in the courtroom.

"Mr. and Mrs. Martin, I would like to caution you, if I hear a murmur that you have even thought of taking this child again without Ms. Stevens's consent, I will make sure you are prosecuted to the full extent of the law. Do you understand me?"

"Yes, Your Honor," Edward answered in a growl. Boldly, he added, "I would like to ask that the court request, each year, a full financial review of my grandson's trust fund."

"Mr. Martin, based on what I have seen, your concerns are noted but unfounded. This court does not need to monitor Ms. Stevens's finances or your grandson's. However, if you have questions or would like to offer your expertise, I suggest you find a way to ask Ms. Stevens. Nicely. One last thing, Mr. Martin, if you want to spend time with your grandson, you will need to develop a relationship with Ms. Stevens."

Judge Roy banged her gavel. "Court is adjourned."

*A*bby exhaled, unaware she had been holding her breath. She reached for Devin. Cari placed him in her arms. Tears of relief streamed down her cheeks. It was over, Devin was coming home with her, forever. Shane wrapped his arms around the woman and boy. Everyone was talking at once. It was hard to think straight. Abby saw Edward and Louise sitting at the table, shoulders slumped in defeat.

She walked over to them. "Edward, Louise, would you like to hold Devin before we leave for Loudon?"

Louise looked up through her tears and Edward's icy glare sliced through her.

"Make no mistake, young lady, we will be keeping an eye on you." Their wooden chairs scraped the hard floor, and they left without a backward glance at Devin.

Abby shook it off; this was their issue, not hers. "Kyle, how soon can we petition for adoption?"

Kyle smiled. "I've already started the paperwork. But for now, go have a celebratory lunch with your friends and then go home."

Shane was waiting for Abby. Pulling them into the security of his arms, he said, "Are you ready to celebrate?"

"I'm more than ready. But first I want to talk to your family."

Cari and Ray were gathering up Devin's toys and other items.

"Well, everyone, didn't you have anything better to do than drive out here and hang out in a courtroom this morning?" Abby stood in the middle of the family, happiness radiating in her smile.

Kate hugged Abby and announced, "Do you think you could keep us away? Your part of our family, and this is what family does for each other."

Abby couldn't believe what she was hearing. "Well, I didn't expect this, but I'm so glad you were here. Since you made the trip, the least I can do is buy lunch. Is anyone hungry?"

Everyone started to talk at once about where they should eat—after all, they were near the ocean, and seafood was the obvious choice. Abby smiled to herself, enjoying being a part of a large extended family. Devin snuggled into her shoulder and promptly fell asleep. Together, Abby and Shane stepped into the hot summer sun.

25

*I*t was pouring when Shane stopped at What's Perkin'. It had been several weeks since Abby had been awarded full custody of Devin, and Shane was ready for the next step toward their future. He walked in, shaking raindrops from his coat. Cari was at the counter savoring a cup of coffee, grateful the lunch rush was over.

"Hey, Mom. Where's Kate?"

"She had an appointment, so I'm holding down the shop. What brings you by, did you want some lunch?" Cari studied her son. Years of experience told her to bide her time; he'd open up when he was ready.

"You don't have to feed me every time I stop in. I know you worry about me eating right." A gleam came to Shane's eye. He peeked in the display case. "It looks like you've got some lemon cake. I guess I could manage a slice."

Cari cut a double slice of the sweet confection.

"Shane, how is Abby doing now that everything has gone back to a new normal?"

He looked up at his mother, fork poised halfway to his

mouth. "She's amazing," he said before he polished off the last crumbs.

Cari stated, "You know Devin means the world to her. Everything she does has his best interest first, even before her needs."

"Mom, don't beat around the bush. What are you trying to say?" He put his fork down, giving his full attention to his mother.

"Shane, you've never brought a girl home for me to meet. I don't know if you've ever had a long-term relationship. If you're not ready to be serious about Abby and Devin, don't string her along. I love you, son, but I've been a single mother, and I can tell you it's hard. To be blunt, are you in love with Abby?" She spoke quietly but deliberately.

*S*hane wasn't surprised his mother would question his intentions. She was right; he hadn't introduced any of his dates to her. Of course, she would empathize with Abby, a single parent who was doing the best she could to raise a child without a permanent support system.

He stated a direct and simple answer: "I'm in love with Abigail Stevens and I intend to ask her to marry me and convince her to let me adopt Devin and raise him as my son." He watched his mother closely as his news registered. She jumped up and pulled him close.

"I'm so happy for you, for all of you. When do you plan to ask her?" Mom wiped away the tears that filled her eyes.

"At the moment, she's enjoying every day with Devin.

But I'm ready, and I don't want to wait. But I wanted to tell you first."

Mom grew thoughtful. "I'm glad you came to me. Abby is a great girl, and you are good for each other. Would you stop by the house tonight before you go to her place?"

"How do you know I'm going to Abby's?"

"Shane, do you really think we don't know you're there every night?" Mom suppressed a laugh.

"Well, I figured you knew we were spending a lot of time together, but I thought I was keeping it on the down low." He chuckled.

He glanced at his watch. "Gotta go, Mom. I'll be by around six if that's okay."

Mom offered her cheek for a kiss and waved him out the door, calling after him to drive carefully.

He was relieved that he had told his mother. Humming to himself, he drove to the job site. His life was falling into place better than he dreamed possible.

⁂

Cari was on the back deck, glass of wine in hand when Shane arrived. Ray was puttering in his shop, giving her some time with her son.

"Hey, Mom. I'm gonna grab a beer. Do you want something?"

Cari held up her glass.

"Ah, you're a step ahead of me. Be right back."

Shane dropped into the chair next to her, put his feet up, and took a deep breath. "It's nice out now that the rain stopped. Jeez, it was just about a year ago that that huge pine tree came down and destroyed part of the house."

"It was a rough time for me. It felt like I had lost part of my life. But look how well everything turned out. Ray rebuilt my home and this wonderful deck. And I found love in the process. Funny how life can change in the blink of an eye."

Cari reached into her pocket and pulled out a small black velvet box. She placed it on the armrest and took a sip of her wine.

Shane didn't speak.

"Your father and I met in college, and I fell for him fast and hard. We were engaged before I graduated." Cari looked at Shane through the eyes of love. "In many ways, you are so much like him. When I look at you, it's like seeing your dad." She tapped the tiny box. "I've been thinking about this day for a long time. There were days when I wasn't sure if you would find someone who makes you happy. It's time I pass this to you, for Abby." Cari handed the box to Shane.

He popped open the box and found, nestled in white velvet, a two-carat sapphire surrounded by tiny diamonds. Shane was stunned. "Mom this is your engagement ring from dad. Are you sure you want me to give Abby this ring? You've worn this ring my whole life. I remember the day you moved it to your right hand; it was right after you announced you were asking Ray to move in with you." Shane handed the box back to his mother. "I can't take this."

Cari put her hand up. "Shane, it's time this ring belonged to a new McKenna bride." She smiled through her tears of joy. "Your father would agree with me. So, tuck it away until you're ready."

Cari and Shane sat quietly, each lost in their own thoughts. Ray strolled across the yard, waving as he approached them. She knew he had been watching them from the shop and, once he witnessed the exchange of the box, that was his signal for him to come home.

"Hey, kid. Want to have another beer?" Ray asked as he moved to the back door.

"Nah, I'm going to take off. I need to stop at my place before I head over to Abby's." Shane leaned over and kissed his mom's cheek.

Ray ducked into the house.

"I love you, Mom, and thanks." He patted the bulge in his shirt pocket. "I hope you know how much this means to me."

"I think I have some idea, son. I'll look forward to the big announcement." Cari beamed.

Ray joined them just as Shane leaped down the steps yelling, "See ya later."

"Was he surprised?" Ray asked as he caressed Cari's palm.

Cari nodded slowly. "It's time. I know it never bothered you. Ben would understand and agree this is the right thing." Cari sighed and squeezed Ray's hand.

"Cari Davis, I'm so proud you're my wife." Ray's gentle kiss brushed over her open palm.

"Mr. Davis, you say the sweetest things. I should start dinner; it's getting late."

With a wicked grin he said, "I have an idea. Let's have dessert first?" Ray suggested with a half laugh, brushing his lips on hers.

A small tremor ran through Cari. "Now *that* is a good idea."

🍷

*M*om's engagement ring was safely tucked into his shirt pocket. He had no idea how or when to pop the question, but he was sure when the time was right, he'd know it.

Shane pulled into his driveway and noted Abby's SUV was parked in her usual spot. He was happy to find Abby and Devin splashing at the water's edge. A reflection from the water at the perfect angle created a halo around them. He half ran into the house to take a quick shower and pull on fresh clothes. It was time.

When Abby looked up she waved. He leaned against the doorjamb watching them. His heart was full and he could feel the huge grin on his face.

"Want to come play?" Abby called.

Shane couldn't resist any longer; the words he had been rehearsing in the shower were ready to fly out of his head. He strolled over the grass to where Abby and Devin were playing and desperately hoped the right words would magically form.

"Looks like you two are having fun." Shane squatted down, scooping Devin up in one fluid motion and pulling Abby up too.

"It was stuffy inside, and Devin gave me that look, you know the puppy dog eye gaze, so here we are, splashing in the water." Abby attempted to wipe Devin's feet on the towel.

"Abs, a little dirt isn't going to hurt me. I'm in it all day, remember?" he teased.

"Do you want to head over to my place now? I'll whip up something for dinner."

Shane seized the opening. "Why don't we stay here, have dinner, relax on the deck, and then sleep here?"

"I would need some things for Devin. Since we need to go home, it would be easier to stay there. Rain check?" Abby suggested.

"Sure, another time. Can we sit down for a few minutes? There's something I've been wanting to talk to you about."

Abby gave him a sunny smile and settled Devin in her lap. He dashed into the kitchen, coming back with a sippy cup for Devin and two glasses of sparkling wine.

Abby took a sip, savoring the sweetness on her tongue. "Delicious," she said, watching as he pulled his chair close to her. A nervous giggle escaped. "Shane, what's the matter?"

Ignoring the question, Shane gently took her small hand in his rough, calloused one. He took a deep breath, exhaled slowly, and said, "Abby, I've known you my entire life. The first time I saw you, we were kids. I thought you were just like my sister: annoying. But we grew up. Our lives moved in different directions. Then circumstances brought you back to Loudon. When I saw you, the day we came to work on your house, I didn't think of you as my sister's best friend. I felt like a ton of bricks fell on me. I don't know if I fell in love with you as kids, or a few months ago. But I know, without a doubt, I am hopelessly and deeply in love with you."

Abby's cheeks went pink. Tears filled her eyes. She opened her mouth to say something, but Shane held his finger to her lips, stopping her in mid-thought.

"I've fallen in love with this little boy." He ran a hand over his head. "I can't imagine my life without either of you. You were a part of my past, both of you are my today, and I want you to be my future."

Shane dropped to one knee, pulled the black velvet

ring box from his pocket, and flipped it open. "Abigail Stevens, will you do me the honor and privilege of becoming my wife?"

Tears streamed down Abby's face. "Shane, you want to marry me? Devin and me, we're a package deal."

He wiped the tears from her cheeks. "I wouldn't have it any other way. Abby, you and Devin are my family, and who knows, maybe someday we'll give him a brother or sister or both. You're the only girl I want to spend my life with. So, what do you think? Marry me?"

"Yes!" Abby threw her arms around his neck, squishing Devin between them and sealing her answer with a kiss.

Shane slipped his mother's ring on her finger. It was a perfect fit. It was as if it was made for her.

"This was the engagement ring my father gave my mother. When I told Mom I was going to propose, she insisted I pass it to you. She said it was time for a new McKenna bride to wear it."

Abby held her hand up and watched the sun dance off the stones. "It's beautiful, Shane."

Shane leaned back in his chair, cradling Devin in one arm as he watched his future wife's face glow.

"So, how long do you think it will take to put together a wedding?" Shane caressed her fingers.

"It all depends on what kind of wedding we want to have. Something large? Months. Small and intimate? Weeks," Abby mused.

"Let's call my parents and see what they're doing four weeks from Saturday if that will give you enough time…"

Shane drifted off as Abby smiled in a dreamlike trance. "That will be plenty of time, and I'm sure my soon-to-be family will be happy to help. How do you feel about a lakeside ceremony?"

"Whatever my bride wants, she gets." Shane kissed her again.

"Wait, we can't get married in four weeks. That's when we're throwing a graduation party for Ellie. I don't want to overshadow her special day. What about next spring? I know you don't want to wait, but this is the one time in a girl's life that is to be treasured. We can still have a small wedding and get married by the lake."

Shane looked at Abby and Devin. "If a spring wedding is what you'd like, then that's what we'll do." He couldn't deny Abby anything, but it was going to be a long winter, he thought.

"Can we have a quick dinner and then run by and see your family? I want everyone to share our good news!"

"Of course. Let's grab a pizza and make the rounds." Shane picked up Devin and pulled Abby into his arms for one last kiss before their news went public. "I can't wait to see the looks on everyone's faces when we tell them."

*U*naware that his life was about to change again, Devin patted Shane's cheek and chattered away, telling him a story that only Devin could understand. Abby gazed at the two men in her life. Her mother had been right; she had said that one day Abby would find her way home to where she truly belonged. Moving to Loudon wasn't about a house; it was about coming home to love.

Keep reading for a sneak peek of
in the Loudon Series
The Last First Kiss
Order Here

THE LAST FIRST KISS

Kate slammed the trunk shut, threw a duffle bag into the back seat, and slammed the door too. How could he think she was going to follow him like a lovesick puppy to Crescent Lake? Climbing behind the wheel, she pulled away from the curb, tires screeching in protest. Kate had to focus on driving and cautiously negotiated the car-lined street. Side streets in Providence were always crowded, and this typically didn't bother Kate, but today, each time she'd had to navigate around another parked car, it was like fingernails on a chalkboard.

Finally, Kate reached the highway and put her foot on the gas pedal. She fought back tears, which threatened to spill from her emerald eyes. Her long dark hair was secured in a scarf as the breeze from the open windows tugged at the stray strands. All she could think about was last night and the fight she had with the man she thought was her forever guy.

It had started over a casual dinner, talking about Kate's upcoming interview as an assistant chef in Boston. It was an amazing opportunity. Kate had dreamed of moving to a city after her graduation from culinary school. She had already delayed the interview to spend some time with Donovan Price, the handsome wine salesman from Crescent Lake Winery. They had gone downstate to Newport for the day and sat on a bench overlooking the ocean. It was peaceful. The sky was azure blue, and the blue-green waves crashed against the rocky shoreline. In the midday sun, there was a light salty breeze to keep them cool. The couple held hands, cherishing the moment. They went to dinner at their favorite pub and then it happened. The fight. The couple drove back to Kate's college apartment in stony silence.

Don intended to help her finish packing the last of the boxes. "Kate." Don was going to try again. "Why don't you skip the interview in Boston? I know a couple of restaurant owners, and you could get a job closer to my family's home. We could see each other every weekend. I know during the week it would be tough since I'm on the road, but weekends we could explore the countryside and do whatever."

"Don, I've busted my back the last four years for an opportunity to even get an interview like this, and you want me to cancel and move to a small town I've visited a couple of times, and work where exactly, for someone who hires me as a favor to you? I don't think so." Kate threw books into an open box. "Why did you wait until tonight to bring this up? Were you afraid of what I would say?"

Don was surprised at Kate's anger. To him, this was the next logical step, to live closer and spend more time together, to see if they had what it would take for forever.

"Kate, I'm sorry. I thought you'd be happy to live in the same town instead of stringing a couple of days together every few weeks."

"I'm not angry that you want to spend more time with me, but your solution is for me to relocate. Why don't you move to where I live; is that too much to ask?" Kate's anger was at a rolling boil. With hands on her hips, she faced him. "Are you saying that if I don't move to Crescent Lake or somewhere in close proximity that we're through?"

"That isn't what I said; stop putting words in my mouth. With my sales territory, getting to Boston won't be any easier than Providence. I want to spend more time with you to see where our relationship might go, but we can't do that if we are a couple of hundred miles apart."

"Considering I have no intention of canceling my interview on the off chance that one of your friends will hire me, this conversation is over. I would like you to leave. NOW!"

"Kate, you're overreacting. We can keep seeing each other."

Kate folded the top of the box and shoved it to one side.

"Kate! Look at me. Talk to me!" Don pleaded with her. "I don't want us to break up."

The temperature in the room had plunged with each passing minute. Don made one last attempt. "Kate, please." Getting nowhere, he turned on his heel and left.

Once she heard the door shut, Kate rushed over, turned the deadbolt, and sank to the floor.

Don stood on the other side and could hear the heart-wrenching sobs. They broke his heart. For a long time, he stood there waiting and praying she would open the door. The minutes dragged until the realization hit—Kate wasn't coming after him. With a heavy heart, Don plodded to his car, lost. The only place he could think to go was home to Crescent Lake Winery.

Kate lay curled up on the floor with her cheek on the hardwood and cried until there were no tears left. She pushed up to a half-sitting position and glanced around—shadows had filled the room. How long had she been there and why hadn't Don come back? Slowly, she stood and grasped the table. Once she felt steadier, she slowly crossed the room to the kitchen, opened the refrigerator, illuminating the small room, to find a solitary bottle of water. She opened it and took a long drink. Kate sank into a lawn chair that dominated the middle of the room, thankful she hadn't put it in the car already. She desperately wanted to call her mother. She glanced at her watch, but it was too late; her mom woke up early to open her coffee shop, What's Perkin'. She walked into the bedroom, flopped on the bed, and fell into a dreamless sleep. Her last thought before exhaustion won: she had to get the job in Boston; she didn't have anything left.

To Keep Reading Order Here

Thank you for reading my novel. I hope you enjoyed the story. If you did, please help other readers find this book:

- This book is lendable. Send it to a friend you think might like it so she can discover me too.

- Help other people find this book by writing a review.
- Sign up for my newsletter at http://www.lucindarace.com/newsletter
- Like my Facebook page, https://facebook.com/lucindaraceauthor
- Join Lucinda's Heart Racer's Reader Group on Facebook
- Twitter @lucindarace
- Instagram @lucindraceauthor

OTHER BOOKS BY LUCINDA RACE:

The Crescent Lake Winery Series 2021

Blends

Breathe

Crush

Blush

Vintage

Bouquet

A Dickens Holiday Romance

Holiday Heart Wishes

Holly Berries and Hockey Pucks

Last Chance Beach

Shamrocks are a Girl's Best Friend

Orchard Brides

Apple Blossoms in Montana

The Matchmaker and The Marine

The MacLellan Sisters Trilogy

Old and New

Borrowed

Blue

The Loudon Series

The Loudon Series Box Set

Between Here and Heaven

Lost and Found

The Journey Home

The Last First Kiss

Ready to Soar

Love in the Looking Glass

Magic in the Rain

ABOUT LUCINDA

Award-winning author Lucinda Race is a lifelong fan of romantic fiction. As a young girl, she spent hours reading romance novels and getting lost in the hope they represent. While her friends dreamed of becoming doctors and engineers, her dreams were to become a writer—a romance novelist.

As life twisted and turned, she found herself writing nonfiction but longed to turn to her true passion. After developing the storyline for The Loudon Series, it was time to start living her dream. Her fingers practically fly over computer keys as she weaves stories about strong women and the men who love them. And if she's not writing romance novels, she's reading everything she can get her hands on. Lucinda has published over twenty books.

Made in United States
North Haven, CT
20 July 2022

21604151R00134